THE MASKED MARKSMAN:
DEATH STEALS THE ACT
AND OTHER STORIES

THE MASKED MARKSMAN

DEATH STEALS THE ACT

AND OTHER STORIES

By Emile C. Tepperman

POPULAR PUBLICATIONS • 2024

OVERTURE TO DOOM

THE GIRL with the straw-colored hair had dropped her knife twice, shattering the dignified quiet of the Longmont restaurant with the din of the silver on china; her white, shapely hand shook a little now as she poured cream into her coffee cup. In her eyes there was a look that Ed Race recognized. It was the look of someone who is hunted—in fear of imminent danger.

Ed had been playing Broadway for a month now, and it looked as if he was set for a winter in New York. His acrobatic gun juggling and marksmanship act at the Clyde Theater had been welcomed back with extravagant acclaim by the jaded vaudeville public of the Big Burg. Kindly old Leon Partages, the owner of the Partages Circuit, had renewed his contract at an even higher figure than before; Ed was sitting pretty among friends and admirers. He should have been at the zenith of happiness in the earthly paradise of all vaudeville troupers—a long engagement in New York. But he was really down in the dumps. The same excess of nervous energy which had driven him to delve into criminology as a sideline was making him painfully aware that nothing exciting had happened in a whole month.

On the stage twice a day, Ed Race performed with six heavy forty-five caliber hair-trigger revolvers, performing feats of marksmanship and split-second drawing and shooting that

would have made any of the legendary Texas bad men spit with envy; off the stage, he always carried two of those guns in the twin holsters beneath his armpits. He was licensed to operate as a private detective in a dozen states, and the fees for those licenses set him back a fat sum annually. Yet he never tried to make a profit out of them.

And somehow, he always managed to attract trouble. Those who knew him often wondered at his uncanny ability to be around when things happened. They said it was something psychic; that his craving for excitement and danger was like the pull of a magnet or like the force of gravity. And yet, there was more to it than that.

For instance, not one man in a thousand would have noticed

the agitation of that girl with the straw-colored hair. Ed lived at the Longmont whenever he was in town, and took his meals in the Longmont restaurant half the time. While he ate, his alert mind was generally busy studying, cataloguing and card index-ing the other diners.

The girl was a stranger here and therefore interested him. She was undoubtedly pretty, not over twenty-two, he judged; and expensively dressed. Her black suede handbag, which matched the modish caracul coat thrown over the back of her chair, seemed to be crammed with something or other that caused it to bulge.

But with all that, there was terror in her eyes....

Ed was seated at a table along the wall, directly facing the next table, at which she sat. Her back was to the main entrance from the hotel lobby, and she did not see the two men who entered, stood for a moment in the doorway, then spied her and started across the room purposefully.

But Ed saw them, and disliked them at once. They were both heavy set, square jawed and square footed, grim. They both wore dark overcoats, nondescript ties, and there was little to distin-guish between them as to attire, except that one had on a derby, and the other a slouch hat.

The girl had finished her coffee, and had taken a powder compact from her purse, closing the purse carefully before beginning to dab the powder on her face with the pink little puff. The two men glanced sideways at each other, nodded as if in confirmation of some unspoken thought, and ranged up behind her chair. In their position, they were facing Ed now, but they paid no attention to him. Their faces now reflected the smug satisfaction that a cat must feel when it is sure that its mouse cannot escape, and watches for the victim to attempt to scurry away to safety before dropping a heavy paw on it.

And now the girl saw them—reflected in the mirror of her compact!

ED SAW her start, saw her body stiffen as she let the powder puff drop from suddenly nerveless fingers into the dregs of the coffee. She seemed frozen, unable to move, under the spell of fear.

The man in the derby tapped her on the shoulder with a thick forefinger. "Well, Miss Sellers," he said loudly enough for Ed to hear, "it looks like we've caught up with you at last!"

A shudder ran through the girl's frame, and she snapped the compact closed. She half turned in her chair, looked up at the two men, and attempted a cool stare.

"I—I don't know what you mean," she said shakily. M-my name is—Smith. Mary S-Smith."

The man in the derby grinned, and winked at his companion. "Smith, huh! You can't pull that stuff on us. This is you, ain't it?"

Out of his breast pocket he pulled a photograph, thrust it in her face. "If you ain't Mimi Sellers, I'm a baboon. We traced you right from Pennsylvania Station—found the Paramount Cab driver that brought you here. You ought to've doubled around a little. You're Mimi Sellers, see?" He bent over her, gripped her shoulder hard, so that she winced. "And your uncle is here in town, too. He's waitin' for you at the Queen Hotel, and you're comin' with us. You better come quiet if you don't want to get hurt!"

The girl's face was gray. "I tell you," she protested feebly, "I'm Mary Smith. I—"

The man shook her hard, growled: "Lay off that stuff!" He half dragged her up from the chair. "You—"

He stopped, stared at Ed Race, who had arisen from his table, and was stepping over toward them.

Ed affected not to notice the two men. He smiled at the girl, said to her genially: "Hello, Miss Smith. Aren't the mosquitoes pesky these days?"

She glanced up at him, startled, and then smiled in sudden relief, understanding that he was coming to her rescue.

Ed swung his eyes to the two men, who were staring at him, open-mouthed. He frowned at them; let his glance rest on the derby wearing one's huge paw, which still clamped the girl's shoulder.

"Miss Smith is an old friend of mine," he said softly. "You two men are creating a disturbance, and annoying her. If you aren't out of here in one minute by that clock over there, I'll throw you both out!"

His cold gray eyes swiveled from one to the other.

The man in the derby took his hand from the girl's shoulder under Ed's gaze. "Looka here!" he blustered. "Who you think you are? We're depitty sheriffs from Omega County, Georgia, and we got a warrant for the arrest of this here woman, Mimi Sellers! You aimin' to interfere with the law?"

Ed grinned at them. "Sounds fishy to me, my friend. A Georgia warrant is no good in New York, and if you're deputy sheriffs, you ought to know it. Let's see that warrant!"

The man in the derby turned to his companion, said queerly: "Show him the warrant, Bastine."

Bastine had his eyes riveted on Ed. "Uh-huh," he said. "Sure I will." His hand went to the inside pocket of his overcoat.

Ed grinned tightly. He moved with all the speed and eye defying swiftness that characterized him on the stage. His left hand flicked out, seized Bastine's wrist in a powerful, punishing grip, wrenched and twisted. Bastine's hand came away from inside his coat, clutching an automatic.

Ed was grinning thinly as he twisted the man's arm without seeming to exert any undue effort. Bastine's face went gray with pain; he uttered a gasp, and let the automatic fall from his hand.

Ed shoved him away, hard, while his right hand thrust out, caught the gun before it reached the ground. He was used to juggling six revolvers at a time on the stage. This was child's play.

His thumb flicked off the safety of the automatic and he leveled it at the derby wearing man, who already had a gun in his hand.

"Drop it!" Ed clipped.

The man dropped the gun. Bastine was crouching now, his teeth bared in a snarl, while Ed covered them both. The girl was watching the whole thing with wide eyes.

THE HALF dozen diners in the room had stopped to stare almost unbelievingly at this bit of gunplay in a restaurant in the heart of New York City. Several waiters were crowding as close as they dared. They all knew who Ed was, and naturally were glad to see him get the upper hand.

Ed kept his eyes on the two, motioned to Panesi, the head-waiter, who had bustled up. "The cops, Nick!" he ordered.

Panesi glared balefully at the two snarling men. "Sure, sure, Signor Race. I getta da cops. Queek!"

He turned to rush out, but the girl suddenly jerked out of her frightened lethargy, snatched at Ed's sleeve.

"No, no, please!" she exclaimed urgently. "Not the police!"

Bastine's mouth twisted in a leer. "Well, wise guy," he said to Ed. "What about your Miss Smith now?"

Ed called out: "Hey, Nick! Never mind. Come back here!"

Panesi hesitated, turned and came back reluctantly.

Ed frowned at the girl. "If these men are really deputy sher-iffs—"

"You bet we are!" the one in the derby growled. "Here," he pulled back his coat, exhibited a shield, "take a look. I don't know who you are, but you sure cooked this dame's hash. She's Mimi Sellers all right, and we got a warrant for her all right—"

"Then why did you pull a gun on me when I asked to see it?" Ed demanded, puzzled.

Bastine spoke up. "We thought you was one of these here New York gunmen what we've been reading about. I guess we was right," he added ruefully. "You sure can scrap!"

The one in the derby started to bluster. "We was going to take her to her uncle, and give her a break by not calling in the New York police. But now, it's the works for her. Here's the warrant—" he extended his hand, and Bastine, under Ed's watchful gaze, gingerly pulled out a folded sheet of paper which he unfolded and held up for Ed to read.

It was a warrant of extradition, without mistake, and it was signed by the governor of New York. It charged that one, Mimi Sellers, was a fugitive from justice from the state of Georgia, and that she was wanted there on a charge of larceny, burglary and embezzlement.

"Now," Bastine snarled, "it's *us* that want the cops!" He swung on Panesi. "Go get 'em, you!"

Panesi glanced questioningly at Ed, who shook his head slightly in the negative, and winked. Panesi smiled sourly, and made for the door. Ed knew that he would stall around outside and return to say that he couldn't find a policeman. Panesi, as well as all the waiters and help in the Longmont, was an enthusiastic admirer of Ed Race, and sought every opportunity to please him.

Ed didn't know why he was still interested in helping the girl after her virtual admission that she was a criminal of some sort. Perhaps it was the hunted look in her eyes; perhaps it was the dislike he had taken at sight to these two blustering minions of the law.

"All right," he said to them. "Maybe you are honest-to-goodness deputy sheriffs. And maybe that is a real warrant you have there. But just the same, this young lady is Mary Smith, and you can't extradite her unless you prove her identity. I—"

He turned to her, and broke off, open-mouthed, staring at the girl's empty chair. He and the two men had been so busy that they hadn't watched her. And now she was gone....

BASTINE SWORE luridly. The derby wearing man swung his eyes about the restaurant, and started to run frantically toward the street exit, through which he had caught sight of the trim, caracul coated figure of the girl departing swiftly.

The girl had just had time to gain the street. Now she glanced back, saw the deputy sheriff coming after her, and broke into a run through the thick, evening Broadway crowds.

The derby wearing man had almost reached the door when one of the waiters whom he passed deftly extended a foot and tripped him. He went crashing to the floor and the girl outside disappeared in the throng.

Bastine had started after her, too, and he gained the door unhindered, ran out into the street, and looked about helplessly. The derby wearing man was picking himself up from the floor, his face red with anger. The waiter who had tripped him sidled around to Ed, grinned and whispered:

"How'd I do, Mr. Race?"

"Fine, Louis!" Ed beamed at him. "See me later. I'll take care of you."

Panesi, the headwaiter, came back in through the hotel entrance, and announced:

"I'm ver-ry sor-ry. But I no can find da cops!"

The guests were crowding around, having forgotten their food. Halloran, the redheaded house detective of the Longmont, pushed through, and eyed Ed and the derby-wearing man with a bilious eye.

"What the hell's goin' on here?" he demanded. He glared at

Ed. "One o' these days we'll ask you to move, Mr. Race. This hotel hasn't been peaceful since you came to stay with us!"

Bastine came back in through the street door, lugging a patrolman. He pointed dramatically at Ed. "That's the guy!" he barked. "He helped the dame to escape. I want him arrested!"

The bluecoat looked sheepishly at Ed. "What's it about, Mr. Race? He claims you helped a fugitive from justice to escape."

Ed shrugged, handed the automatic back to Bastine. "Sorry if I messed up the works for you," he grinned. "How was I to know you were deputy sheriffs? You barged in here like a couple of yeggs."

"I don't care what you knew!" the derby wearing one roared. "You obstructed justice, an' you're gonna get locked up! Take him in, officer!"

The bluecoat looked pained. "These two men are making a charge against you, Mr. Race. I guess I'll have to take you down to the precinct house. Accordin' to the rule book I got to make an arrest whenever it's demanded by a citizen. Of course," he turned and glowered at the two sheriffs, "if this should prove to be a false arrest you two birds will pay through the nose!"

"Go ahead!" Bastine shouted. "You'll see if it's a false arrest. Take him in!"

The cop shrugged, looked helplessly at Ed, who nodded at him. "You got to do your duty, Mason. Come on, let's go."

On the way out, he glanced at Halloran, the Longmont house detective. Halloran was smirking with satisfaction. "You had it coming to you a long time, Race. I'll be glad to be rid of you. Want me to send your bags over to the county jail?"

"Go to hell!" Ed told him.

NIGHT COURT was crowded. Peering out from the detention room, which opened into the courtroom, Ed could see lawyers, bondsmen, and curiosity seekers jamming in through the double doors. The seats were all taken, as usual. Court attendants strutted up and down the aisles, and a small group of men were clustered about the magistrate's bench, waiting to get a word with him.

The clerk bustled over and shooed them away—all but two men who he nodded to deferentially. One was fat little Leon Partages, the owner of the vaudeville circuit for which Ed worked; the other was Franklin Harrison, tall, gray-haired, dignified, with a look of supercilious distaste on his handsome, patrician features. Franklin Harrison was one of the most renowned members of the bar in the State of New York. He had been a justice of the Supreme Court himself, and had retired to private practice some years ago, handling only work of a nature that commanded hundred thousand dollar fees. He was the attorney for the Partages Circuit, and Ed grinned at the thought that good old Leon had dragged Harrison down here to night court to take care of the case. It was a safe bet that Harrison hadn't been inside a magistrate's court in the last twenty years.

The court clerk conducted the lawyer and Leon up to the judge's bench, and around in back. While spectators gaped, and Ed watched, amused, from the detention room where he stood next to a couple of drunk-and-disorderlies, the magistrate arose and shook hands with the great Franklin Harrison, and then acknowledged the lawyer's introduction of Leon Partages.

The three whispered for a few minutes, and then the magistrate beckoned to the clerk, gave him some instructions. The clerk nodded, picked out a sheaf of papers from a batch on his desk. Then he tapped on the desk with a gavel for order, and called out:

"Case of Edward Race! Short affidavit signed by Lewis Bastine and Theodore Ringler!"

The attendant in charge of the detention room nodded to Ed. "Looks like you got drag, guy—being called first!"

Ed walked up to the bench, grinned at Leon Partages, who shook his head disapprovingly. Franklin Harrison scowled. "This your man?" he asked Partages.

Partages bobbed his head. "Eddie," he reproved, "I never saw anybody who could scare up more trouble than you!"

Harrison said to Ed: "I've asked the judge to adjourn this for a week. I hope I can get you straightened out by that time. If we can find this girl, and turn her over to the complainants, they'll drop the charge—"

"Thanks," Ed said drily. "I'd rather not do it that way."

HARRISON'S SCOWL grew deeper, while the magistrate watched them. "Look here, Race, if I'm going to take care of this for you, you'll do as I say! Now just keep quiet!"

He nodded to the clerk, who called out: "The complainants in this case will step forward!"

From one of the benches the two deputy-sheriffs arose, and came up beside Ed and the attorney.

The clerk intoned: "Edward Race, you are charged with obstructing justice, with aiding a fugitive to escape, and with simple assault. How do you plead to all these charges—guilty or not guilty?"

Before Ed could answer, Harrison broke in suavely; "If your honor please, I suggest that this whole matter may be straightened out by our producing the young woman whom these officers are seeking. I have engaged a firm of private detectives who are even now combing the city—"

Ed broke in vehemently: "Excuse me, your honor. Being the defendant in this case, I have some rights. I don't want this man as my attorney unless he handles the case my way. I don't believe the young lady in question was guilty of any of the crimes charged against her. I think these two deputy sheriffs are a couple of crooks, and I want a chance to prove it. If you'll fix bail for me, I'll be glad to put it up, and then go about this in my own way!"

The magistrate looked perplexed, glanced at Franklin Harrison for guidance. The great attorney became apoplectic. "Well, I never!" he exclaimed. He turned to Leon Partages. "See here, Mr. Partages, am I handling this, or are you going to allow this scatterbrained actor to get himself all tangled up with the law? He doesn't—"

Leon Partages spread his hands deprecatingly. "I'm sorry, Mr. Harrison, but anything that Eddie does is okay with me. I've seen him in action plenty times before. Don't worry. He knows what he's about."

"I want those detectives of yours called off, Harrison!" Ed barked. "At once!"

Harrison glanced apologetically at the magistrate, and said

to Partages: "Very well. Then I withdraw from this case. I will not be insulted—"

"If you withdraw from this case," Partages told him flatly, "you withdraw as the attorney for the Partages Circuit."

HARRISON HESITATED, gulped. The Partages Circuit paid him more than sixty percent of his annual income. "Very well," he snapped. "I'll handle this your way, Race. But don't blame me if you end up in the penitentiary!"

He turned to the bench, once more suave. "If your honor please, I will ask that you adjourn this case till next week and parole the defendant in my custody. I will be personally responsible for his appearance."

The magistrate nodded. "Case adjourned for one week. Defendant paroled in custody of counsel. Next case!"

The two deputy sheriffs started to protest. "Wait a minute, judge!" Bastine shouted. "We won't be here next week. We can't stay that long—"

"Next case!" the judge snapped.

The attendant pushed the two protesting deputies out of the way, and Ed, grinning, took Partages by the arm, led him up the aisle. Harrison said goodbye to the judge, and followed them sourly.

Ed's eyes narrowed as he noted a young woman in a heavy black veil, seated at the end of one of the benches, near the door. Her hands were in her lap, and he thought he recognized their long, white slimness. But he said nothing, continued on out of the courtroom, and into the street.

Outside, Partages motioned to his limousine, drawn up at the curb, alongside the "no parking" sign.

"Come on, Mr. Harrison, the three of us'll go have a drink and talk this over. You don't want to get sore at me. I've known Eddie a long while, and I always back him up—the same as he's backed me up many a time." He pushed Harrison, slightly mollified, into the car, the door of which the chauffeur had opened, and turned to Ed. "Come on, Eddie, boy—"

"Sorry, Mr. Partages. I've got some things to attend to. You see that Harrison calls off his detective agency, will you?"

Partages looked at him for a long minute. "All right," he finally gave in. "I guess you know what you're up to, Eddie. Only don't go and get yourself arrested again. It's lucky tonight is Sunday and there's no show; or look, we'd been without your number at the Clyde."

"I'll be careful, Mr. Partages," Ed told him.

"This girl," the vaudeville owner persisted. "You know her well, maybe?"

Ed grinned. "I never saw her before tonight."

"And you took a chance on going to jail for her!"

"I'm sure she's not as bad as those hick deputies from Georgia want to make her out. There's something wrong with the picture, and I'm going to find out what it is."

"Good luck to you then, Eddie. And if you need me for anything you just call up. I haven't forgotten the things you've done for me."

Ed watched the limousine roll away, and then turned in time

to see the two disgruntled deputies coming out of the court-house.

They strolled down a few feet, and stood, talking and leaning against the building, their eyes on Ed.

Ed began to walk away slowly, across Fifty-Fourth in the direction of Broadway, and they immediately started after him. He glanced back, stopped.

They stopped, too.

Behind them, he could see the slim form of the veiled girl emerge from the court, stand uncertainly on the sidewalk.

Ed walked directly back toward the two sheriffs. They stood their ground. When he came up close to them, Ed said: "Do you bozos intend to follow me all night?"

They grinned. "You bet!" the derby wearing Ringler said. "We're stickin' to you till we find out where you got that dame cached. We daren't go back to the Queens Hotel and tell her uncle that we lost her."

"You'd do much better," Ed told them mildly, "by turning around and going right back toward the court. You'd stand a better chance of finding her than by trailing me. But," he sighed, "I don't suppose you'll believe me."

"You're right!" Bastine said. "You bet we don't believe you. You and Mimi Sellers was hooked up to hoodwink us. Imagine— claimin' her name was Smith!"

RINGLER THRUST his jaw out at Ed. "An' let me tell you, mister, there ain't no law to prevent us followin' you around—as long as we don't interfere with you. We're stickin' till we catch that dame. Sooner or later you got to pay a visit to where you got her holed up."

Ed shrugged. "Have it your way, gentlemen." He pushed past them, toward the courthouse. "Excuse me. I see someone I know."

He made for the slim caracul coated figure near the courthouse steps, and the two sheriffs sauntered after him slowly.

The girl saw him approach, saw the two men behind him, and seemed to be in a quandary as to what to do. Before she could make up her mind, Ed had come up beside her, taken her arm.

"It's all right," he said. "Those two Sherlocks won't think I'd have the nerve to meet you right under their noses."

She obeyed his hand on her elbow, allowed him to help her into a cab at the curb. "Drive uptown," he ordered.

He glanced back through the rear window, chuckled as he saw his two shadows getting into another cab.

He faced forward again, glanced at the girl, and saw that she had raised her veil.

"Why did you come down here?" he asked her. "You took an awful chance."

She shuddered. "I—I had to find out—what was going to happen to you. You were so k-kind to come to my aid. I—I couldn't b-bear to see you go to jail. If that had happened, I w-was going to give myself up."

"Attagirl!" Ed praised her. "Now let's hear the story of your criminal career. How come you got the bloodhounds of the law on your trail?"

"It's my uncle," she told him, "my Uncle George. He's been

my guardian. He's the boss of the political machine in Omega County, and besides that he's the surrogate. When dad and mother were killed in an auto accident about ten years ago, he took over the management of the estate. There wasn't much cash, but there was the collection of Russian jewels which dad had built up. There are some pieces in that collection which are priceless. They come from the crown jewels."

Ed eyed her bulging handbag. "Your dad was a collector?"

"Yes. He'd been American Consul in Moscow, and he put all his money into buying those pieces. Well, Uncle George lost all his money not so long ago, and I began to see men come into the house late at night, and I found out he was selling the collection bit by bit. He could do anything he liked about it, because he was only accountable to himself, being surrogate as well as executor of dad's will, and my guardian.

"I protested to him, and he got very angry, and had two alien-ists come in and examine me, and they said I was insane. So Uncle George had me put away in the Omega County Home for Mental Incompetents. That was two years ago, before I came of age. Last week I tied some bed sheets together, shinned out the window, and escaped. I hitchhiked home, and stole into the house. I knew where the jewels were kept, so I took them, and got dressed up in all my best clothes, that I found in the closets. And here I am—with the jewels. N-now they w-want to t-take me back. Uncle George will have me locked up in the insane asylum for the rest of my life, and he'll sell them all."

"H'mm, very interesting," Ed remarked. "Uncle George must be a very nice man."

The cab driver turned around, said: "Look, mister, you said to drive uptown. Well, did you mean Forty-Second, or Ninety-Sixth, or the Bronx, maybe? I like to be accurate about them things."

Ed glanced out, saw that they were just passing Times Square. Looking back he saw the cab in which the two bloodhounds were following, close behind. They were sticking grimly.

"There's a cab following us," Ed told the driver. "Do you think you could shake them—for a ten dollar bill?"

"For a sawbuck I could try, mister," the driver said. "For twenty I could guarantee results."

Ed sighed. "All right, Captain Kidd."

At once the driver swung right into Forty-Fourth Street, slowed down and approached the green light at Sixth Avenue. Behind them came the other cab.

Ed's driver called back: "This is an old trick, mister, that's easy worth twenty to watch. It calls for perfect timing."

He rolled up close to the corner, and just as the traffic light began to change, he made a left turn into Sixth, in front of the traffic cop, who waved him on, but held up a hand to stop the cab behind.

Ed looked back, grinned to see the two sheriffs darting out of their taxi, paying off in a hurry, and starting out on foot.

The driver asked: "Did it work, mister?"

"It did. Now show a little speed. They're coming after us on foot."

"Okey doke, mister!" The driver made a left turn at Forty-

Fifth, raced across to Broadway. "I guess that loses 'em, huh? Where to now?"

"Queens Hotel," Ed told him. "And here's your twenty—with two extra for the fare. You did fine!"

The girl beside him asked breathlessly: "W-what are you going to do? Uncle George is at the Queens!"

"That's right, Mimi. We're going to talk to your uncle George. I have an idea he needs a little talking to!"

BUT AT the Queens Hotel Ed was informed that Mr. George Sellers was out, had left word that he would not be back till midnight. It was nine thirty.

They went back to the cab, which had waited outside, and Ed said: "To the Longmont, Captain Kidd. It looks like you're hired for the night."

"I only hope," Captain Kidd replied, "that some other goofs take the notion to trail you, mister. Twenty bucks a crack is better than regular hacking—and I know lots more tricks."

At the Longmont, Ed told Mimi to put her veil down again, and took her in through the side entrance, and up to the fourth floor, where his room was.

Ed fitted the key into the lock of his door, pushed it open, and stared at the tableau in the lighted room. Halloran, the redheaded house detective, sat in the only chair in the room, with his hands clasped awkwardly behind his neck. His face was red, and he was glaring at the dapper, black-haired man who sat on the bed and covered him with an automatic.

As Ed appeared in the doorway, the dapper man swung the

automatic so that it covered Ed, too, and said genially: "Come in. We've been expecting you."

Halloran started to move, and the dapper man swung the automatic in his direction again, his eyes snapping viciously. "Keep those hands behind your neck!"

Halloran subsided.

The dapper man looked at Ed. "Well, I thought I told you to come in. Or would you like to be found with a bullet between the eyes, right across your threshold?"

"I'll come in," Ed said mildly. "I was just wondering if your name was George Sellers." As he spoke he tried to nudge the girl behind him away from the door, but she exclaimed: "It's Uncle George!"

Uncle George smiled thinly. "This is indeed a surprise, Mimi! Come in, too. I had anticipated a good deal of trouble in making Mr. Race, here, disclose your whereabouts to me."

Ed and the girl moved into the room, and Ed closed the door behind them.

Halloran, with his hands still behind his neck, said sheepishly: "This guy was fumbling around your door, Race, so I braced him. And he yanks a gat on me, and marches me in here!"

"Too bad, Halloran," Ed said, his eyes twinkling. "It's terrible how they treat detectives nowadays."

The dapper man got up from the bed, keeping his eyes on Ed. He moved around behind Halloran, put a hand in front of the detective, into his shoulder holster, and drew out the big service revolver that the house dick carried there. Then, still keeping

Ed covered with the silenced automatic, Sellers raised the big revolver, brought it down hard.

The house detective grunted, slumped in the chair, then fell to the floor and did not move.

"That," said Sellers softly, "disposes of him, so that I can do my business with you." His automatic was fixed unwaveringly on Ed's stomach. "Mimi!" he ordered sharply. "Give me that handbag. You have the jewels in it?"

"I won't!" she flashed. "They were Dad's, and they're mine now!"

Sellers did not raise his voice. "Mimi," he told her, "I'm a desperate man. With those jewels that you took, was a list of all the items that I received from the estate. Over a dozen of those items have already been sold. I want that list. With it, you could send me to jail. Can you imagine me going to jail? Of course not. Believe me, Mimi, I would just as soon kill you and your big friend here, as well as this house detective, as go to jail. Now, do you understand how desperate I am? I want those jewels, and I want that list!"

All the time that he talked to Mimi he kept his eyes and his gun glued to Ed....

THERE WAS a cold, desperate glint in those eyes that told Ed the man meant every word he said. Men like this always became cold, dangerous killers when they stood in danger of losing the prestige and respect they had built up for themselves on a foundation of apparent respectability.

But the girl, Mimi, stood her ground. Apparently she didn't think that her Uncle George would go as far as actually killing her. In spite of the example of Halloran, who lay supine on the floor, she clutched her bag tightly against her breast. "No, no! I won't! You don't dare shoot!"

Sellers' lips tightened. The automatic swung just a little away from Ed, centered on the girl. "I hate to do this Mimi. I had hoped that Ringler and Bastine would be able to bring you here without publicity. But this blundering fool spoiled that. Now you must die!"

Even as he said the last, his finger started to contract on the trigger.

And Ed Race swung into that swift, blinding action which had dazzled the eyes of spectators at the Clyde.

He shouted: "Hey!" and drew the involuntary attention of George Sellers to himself. Sellers' gun swung toward him, as Ed's hand darted in and out, with lightning swiftness, from his holster.

At the same instant, Ed's body went into a double back somersault, just like the one that he did on the stage. At the theatre, Ed came out of that somersault with six guns in the air, caught them one at a time as they came down, and shot out the lights of candles thirty feet away.

Sellers' silenced automatic spat wickedly once, twice. The slugs missed Ed completely, because his body was in motion. But the heavy lead pill from his own .45 did not miss. It caught Sellers right between the eyes, hurled him back against the wall with a sickening crash. His body crumpled, slumped over onto Halloran's.

Ed Race came to his feet against the opposite wall, stood

23

looking down at the man he had killed. The girl was still standing where she had been when the shooting started, rooted to the spot, still clutching her handbag.

Ed took the bag from her fingers, opened it and withdrew a chamois bag from within it. He undid the string that held it together at the top, and poured out into his hand a dazzling collection of pearls and diamonds, each with a tag on it. Among the stones was a small, folded piece of paper, which he opened:

ACCOUNTANT'S LIST OF
ITEMS IN SELLERS ESTATE

Placed in the hands of George Sellers, executor without bond. Checked by Hayes, Hayes, Hinkle & Murphy: Certified Public Accountants.

"This is the list that would have sent him to jail," Ed said somberly.

The girl clutched at his sleeve. "I—I didn't think it meant anything! I—I almost threw it away!"

"It's a good thing you didn't. It forced your Uncle George out into the open. If it hadn't been for this list, he could just have sat tight and waited for you to be picked up for robbing your own estate!"

Halloran, on the floor, stirred, and moaned. Outside, someone was pounding on the door.

Halloran opened his eyes, felt the weight of Sellers' body on him, exclaimed: "Omigawd! What's this!"

"That," Ed told him as he went to open the door, "is the cue for you to start playing at house detective again!"

DEATH BETWEEN THE ACTS

ED RACE'S big, capable hands were wrapped tight around the rim of the steering wheel, and he kept his eyes straight ahead as he swung into Biscayne Boulevard, making seventy-two, with his foot down almost to the floorboard on the accelerator.

He had covered the sixty miles from Palm Beach to Miami in forty minutes, without being stopped by any traffic policemen. Traffic was light at this time of the evening, and he saw only a single sedan ahead. It was a large, seven-passenger car, and it had been making as good time as Ed himself, all the way from Hollywood, which was about twenty miles north of Miami. Ed had tried to pass it a couple of times, but the speed its driver was making had prevented that.

Now the car ahead slowed up, and Ed guessed that they, too, were preparing to make the turn into the causeway which led across the bay to Miami Beach. And it was just at that instant that the thing happened.

The left-hand rear-door of the sedan was suddenly flung open, and a girl leaped out, hit the pavement and rolled in the path of Ed's car, skirts billowing high over her shapely legs.

Ed clamped down hard on the brake. His car screamed to a stop within a foot of the girl, who was already scrambling to her feet. The car out of which she had leaped lurched to a halt, and a stocky man jumped out from the driver's seat, ran back toward her. The girl, her pretty face twisted into a mask of terror in the glare of Ed's headlamps, saw the stocky man, uttered a shriek, and started to run aimlessly. She stumbled, fell, and got to her feet again. Apparently she had been hurt in her leap from the car in spite of the fact that they had slowed down considerably. But she seemed desperate, frantic.

The stocky man caught up to her in three strides. His face was cool, impassive, as he seized her arm and, without saying a word, started to drag her back toward the sedan. The girl screamed and tried to scratch her captor's face. Without change of expression the stocky man struck her in the face with his clenched fist, and she wilted, hanging limply in his arm.

Ed had the door of his car open by this time, and he sprang out, shouted: "Hey, you!" and raced toward them.

The stocky man paid no attention to Ed, but made steadily for the sedan. Out of the big car another man hopped. This one was little, thin, with a single wisp of nondescript-colored hair on an otherwise bald dome. The little man gazed at Ed with a queer, bird-like stare, and whipped a hand out of the side pocket of his linen jacket. The hand was balled around the butt of an automatic, and the automatic pointed at Ed.

"Stay outta this, mister," the little man said. "It's none of your business!"

Ed slowed up. He was only a few feet from the muzzle of that gun, and its holder spoke as if he meant to use it. The stocky man was already bundling the girl back into the car when she seemed to awake from her lethargy, and screamed again. She began to

shriek and scratch and kick, and for a second her captor was taken aback. In that second, she broke his hold on her, started to run toward Ed. The stocky man cursed, came after her, and caught her again, just alongside of Ed Race. The two of them were now between Ed and the little man with the gun, and Ed took advantage of the situation, threw an arm around the stocky man's throat, lifted him by the seat of the pants, and fairly hurled him at the man with the gun.

The two of them went down in a welter of arms and legs, and the automatic slid out of the little man's hand, while its owner slumped under the body of the man whom Ed had thrown.

The stocky fellow got to his feet, crouched, and rushed at Ed. Ed met him with a stiff uppercut that sent him back into the side of the sedan. Then Ed stepped in, picked up the automatic.

The stocky man was feeling in his coat for a gun, but Ed calmly lifted a hard fist to his chin. This time he went out cold. Ed whirled, looking for the girl. She had disappeared!

BISCAYNE BOULEVARD at this point is rather deserted at night. Two cars had passed while the fight was going on, but neither had stopped. Motorists these days aren't anxious to get into brawls that may hold them up, or cause their appearance in court as witnesses.

Ed turned back to the two men. The little man was still slumped down, his head resting on the running board of the car, where it had struck when he fell. The stocky man was stirring, but still unconscious. Ed grinned ruefully. He had mixed in something that was none of his business. For all he knew, these two men might be officers of the law, and the girl might be a felon. Of course, she didn't look like a criminal, and Ed hadn't liked the way the stocky man hit her.

He glanced around, seeking for some possible place where the girl might have disappeared to. There was none. This was the Thirteenth Street Circle, and traffic had to make a wide detour around a monument, then either go on down Biscayne Boulevard toward Flagler Street and the center of town, or else turn left into the causeway.

Opposite was the vast bulk of a department store; on his own side of the street there was a row of stores, all closed for the night. There was literally no place where she could have gone, unless she had taken refuge in one of the darkened store entryways—in which case he could not have missed her bright orange dress. Yet it was not in evidence.

Ed shrugged, carefully wiped his prints from the automatic, then dropped it alongside the unconscious men. Then he got into his own sedan and drove around the circle, swung left onto the causeway. He glanced at his wristwatch, and cursed under his breath. He had lost precious minutes back there. Now he stepped on the accelerator, drove the needle up to sixty, sixty-five. The concrete, three-and-a-half-mile causeway across Biscayne Bay, linking the City of Miami to the City of Miami Beach, was a beautiful piece of construction work. Wide and smooth, it was easy driving, and gave one an opportunity to glimpse the splendor of the view on either side. Far over to the left, one could see the long row of electric lights that marked the Venetian Way, the second of the three causeways across the bay. To the right was the gorgeous skyline of Miami, which reminded Ed almost of New York's own skyline. There were tall buildings and garish lights, and something that looked like the string of lights on a shoot-the-chutes, but which was really the illumination for the aquarium boat anchored along the bay-front of Miami.

Ed paid but scant attention to these things now. His face was tight, as he sped past palatial yachts tied up along the causeway, past the landing field of the Goodyear blimp which had crashed only the other day. He was swinging around the wide curve which approached the first of the two drawbridges in the causeway, when he heard a *chug-chugging* alongside, glanced out the window and saw a grim-faced motorcycle cop motioning him to pull over.

He bit his lip in vexation, slowed down, and came to a stop along the edge of the water. The cop parked the motorcycle just ahead, and came back swaggering, a hand on the holster hanging from his Sam Browne belt.

"Let's have yoah license, mistah," the officer said grimly.

Ed took out his wallet, handed over his driver's license and the card from the Drive-Yourself company.

The cop grunted. "New Yawk, eh? You fellahs seem to think you-all own this here town. This ain't a license to do seventy, mister!"

"Look here, officer," Ed said desperately, "I've got to get to the Miami Beach Dog Track by nine o'clock. It's a matter of life and death. That's why I was tearing up the road."

The officer raised his eyebrows. "Life an' death, eh? How come?"

ED TOOK a crumpled telegram from his pocket. "I was up at Palm Beach tonight, and I got this telegram from an old friend of mine. I tried to reach him by telephone, but he wasn't home. So I hired a car and started to drive here."

The cop took the blank suspiciously, and read it. It was as follows:

DEATH BETWEEN THE ACTS

EDWARD RACE
  C/O FLORIDA THEATER
  PARTAGES CIRCUIT
  PALM BEACH FLA COME AT ONCE MIAMI
BEACH DOG TRACK STOP BRING TEN GRAND
STOP LIFE AND DEATH STOP ODDS ARE TERRIBLE
AGAINST ME BUT ITS LAST CHANCE TONIGHT
STOP COME BEFORE NINE OCLOCK STOP DONT
FAIL STOP I KNOW YOU CAN GET THE MONEY
FROM YOUR BROKERS THEY ARE OPEN TILL
TEN OCLOCK STOP ILL BE WAITING FOR YOU AT
TRACK BUT IF YOU MISS ME REMEMBER ITS LIFE
AND DEATH

CHARLEY WIENER

The cop frowned, read the telegram through a second time. While he was doing this, Ed kept glancing nervously back along the causeway toward Miami. He had at first thought that the officer was after him for the fracas back at Biscayne Boulevard. He had been more or less relieved to learn that he was just being stopped for speeding. Now he feared that some other officer might have discovered the two men at the sedan, and come after him. He said to the cop:

"You ought to know Charley Wiener. Everybody down here knows him. He comes to Miami every year. He owns a string of dogs—"

"Yeah, sure," the cop told him. "I know Charley Wiener. A hell of a nice guy. He goes fishin' right here off the causeway every Sunday night. But I can't figure out what kind of life and

31

death jam he can be in. An' I don't know you. What's this about the Florida Theater at Palm Beach, an' the Partages Circuit?"

Ed looked at his watch. It was twenty-five minutes to nine. He could take ten minutes to explain and still have time to make the track by nine o'clock—provided the cop gave him a break. He explained patiently:

"I'm an actor. I'm working over at the Florida this week. I'll play Hollywood next week, and the Miami Theater the week after. Then I'm booked for the Miami Biltmore over at Coral Gables. I play this circuit every winter. Maybe you've seen my act—The Masked Marksman—"

"Say!" the cop exclaimed. "Are you the Masked Marksman? The guy that juggles those big, forty-five caliber revolvers on the stage, an' does somersaults, an' shoots out candles?"

Ed nodded. "That's me."

The cop sighed. He folded up Ed's license, and handed it back to him. "I saw your act last year. I came every day while you were at the Miami, and I trotted out to Coral Gables every day the week after. Your act is a knockout, Mr. Race. If I could shoot like you, I'd die happy!" He stretched out his hand. "Will you shake with me, Mr. Race?"

At that particular moment, Ed would have kissed him. He took the license, shook hands with the cop.

"My name is Seeley," the officer said. "Tom Seeley. And I'm mighty glad to make your acquaintance, Mr. Race. Anything I can do for you, why just say the word."

"That's white of you," Ed said. "All I want to do is to get

over to the dog track and see what sort of jam Charley is up against—"

"Okay," Tom Seeley said. "You're goin' there—like a gentleman!"

He strode over to his motorcycle, kicked it into life, and straddled it. Then he turned, grinned, and shouted over the barking of his motor: "You're gonna have an escort to the track, Mr. Race. An' talk about speed—you try an' keep up with me!"

He raised an arm, got into motion, and roared out along the causeway.

Ed grinned, shoved his car into gear, and followed. The needle of his speedometer crept up past the seventy mark, touched eighty, slipped past, and hovered around eighty-five. Ahead of him, the motorcycle made a thin streak of speed, its siren shrieking, clearing a path for them.

ALMOST IN the blink of an eyelid they had left the causeway, and were in Miami Beach. Seeley sped down Fifth Street, with Ed hanging close behind him, and swung right on Washington Avenue, heading straight for the dog track. Cars pulled aside to let them pass, and pedestrians stopped to stare, wondering what high-muck-a-muck was being accorded a princely escort to the track.

Ed was chuckling to himself, thinking of the two men he had left lying next to the big sedan on Biscayne Boulevard. He wondered who the girl was, and where they'd been taking her; what sort of desperate frenzy had caused her to leap from the car; and where she had disappeared to. Seeley was about a block ahead of him, and the lights of the dog track had come in sight, when Ed suddenly felt something hard poked into his back. He stiffened, raised his eyes to the rear-vision mirror, and saw the face of the girl he had been thinking about. She was in the rear seat, and her face was white, determined. She said: "Slow up, Mister Race, and let me out. I've got your gun—I got it out of the side pocket. And believe me, I'll shoot if you don't stop!"

Ed exclaimed: "My God! So you were hiding in there all the time? That's where you disappeared to!"

She was hardly more than nineteen, he saw now, and fragilely pretty. Her hair was corn-colored and bobbed, and her face was thin, almost elf-like. She was under some dreadful strain, he could see, and she might shoot from nervousness, if for no other reason.

He said hastily: "Look out for that gun, Miss. It's got a hair trigger. It might go off before you know it!"

The cold muzzle was up against the back of his neck, and he shuddered to think of what he'd look like if the big forty-five exploded now.

"Never mind talking!" the girl grated. "Slow up and let me out!"

Ed applied the brake gently, eased down to fifty, forty, thirty. Seeley and his motorcycle pulled away from them. Ed said: "Listen, Miss, suppose I don't slow up. If you shoot me, the car'll crash and you'll be killed or maimed. You don't dare to shoot."

"Oh, yes I do!" she said vehemently. "If I don't get away, I might as well be dead anyway! You better stop!"

Ed stopped.

"Now," she asked, "where's that ten thousand dollars you said you were taking to the track?"

Ed laughed hollowly. "That was only a gag, sister. You don't think I'd carry ten thousand—?"

He stopped as the gun poked a little harder into his neck. "I want that money. I want it bad enough to—commit—murder for it!"

Her lips were close to his ear as she leaned forward, crouching in the rear, and he caught the faint odor of the perfume she used. The car was still rolling, and he took his foot off the brake, let it continue to roll. "I'll take a chance," he said, grinning. "I don't think you're a killer, sister. I'm not handing over any ten grand to the first girl with a gun that asks me for it. Let's see you shoot."

"All right then. When I count three I'm going to pull the trigger!" In a whisper she said: "One! Two! Th—" She uttered a little groan, threw the gun away, and it fell with a clatter to the floorboard at Ed's feet. Ed pulled his feet out of the way with a jerk, and the hair-trigger exploded with a mighty crash. The slug from the gun smashed out through the right hand door, through the thin metal, leaving a rough, gaping hole in the body.

"I—I couldn't do it!" she moaned, and put her hands up to her face. Her shoulder shook as she sobbed.

Ed groaned, looking ruefully at the hole in the door. "Those guys will charge me damages now! Couldn't you have put the thing down instead of throwing it?"

HE PICKED the gun up, put it into the holster under his right armpit. There already was one gun under his left armpit, and this was its mate. He had taken it out because it made too much of a bulge under his palm-beach jacket. But now he thought he had better wear it. These revolvers were two of the matched six with which he performed each day at the theater. And he never went out without carrying them. In addition to being a headline vaudeville artist, Ed Race had developed a hobby of recent years that helped to lend the touch of excitement to his life which his nervous energy craved. He dabbled in criminology as a sideline, and held licenses to act as a private detective in a dozen states. Few people outside of the theatrical world knew that Ed Race, the private detective, was also the Masked Marksman of vaudeville fame. He always appeared on the stage with a mask, and tried to keep his identity secret so far as possible. For in his career of crime investigation he had made a respectable number of enemies, and he didn't relish the idea of being potted from the orchestra of a theater while he was performing on the stage.

Not that he disliked the thrill of the constant danger. Ed could have retired comfortably on the money he had made in the vaudeville business in the last eight years. The salary he received as a headliner was far too large for him to spend, considering the simple way he lived.

He made no effort to save, or to conserve his funds, yet they seemed to grow in spite of himself, mocking him when he told himself he remained in the vaudeville business because he had to. He knew within himself that he stayed because he couldn't live without the excitement of the theater, without the thunderous applause that greeted his every appearance on the stage.

He gambled with his money in large chunks, invested in

crazy, wildcat schemes, and lent money indiscriminately. Yet his gambles always seemed to be lucky ones, the wildest stocks he bought started paying dividends after he invested in them. Friends to whom he lent cash generally made a comeback and repaid him. So Ed had accumulated more money than he knew what to do with. And if Charley Wiener had asked him for fifty thousand instead of ten, he would have gotten it gladly.

Now, as he holstered the gun, he turned and inspected the girl, who was softly weeping behind him. "I'm in a hurry now, sister," he told her. "But if you'll wait till I take care of my business at the track, maybe I can help you, if you'll tell me what's your trouble. You—"

He stopped as the girl raised her eyes and gasped, pointing ahead of them. Ed looked, saw the single big eye of a motorcycle headlamp bearing down on them.

"It's the policeman!" she gasped. "P-please! D-don't give me away!" And she ducked behind the seat.

Ed frowned, puzzled, and turned to greet Seeley, who pulled up alongside. The cop exclaimed: "What happened, Mr. Race? I all of a sudden saw I was alone, so I come back to look for you!"

"I—er—the ignition went dead," Ed explained. "Fuse blew. It's all right now, though." He went through the motions of fumbling with the fuse under the dashboard. "I wrapped it in silver paper from my cigarette package, and I guess it'll last till tomorrow."

Seeley looked impressed. "Say, that's a good idea, Mr. Race. I never heard of wrapping 'em in silver paper. Fuse once blew on me out on the Tamiami Trail, an' I was stuck in the Everglades all night. Sorry I didn't know that stunt."

"Well, you just remember it for future use. Shall we start again?"

Seeley nodded, swung his cycle around, and headed off. "We'll just make it," he called back.

ED FOLLOWED again, and the girl poked her head up once more. "Please," she said. "I heard everything you said to the policeman about who you were. Will you promise me something? It's terribly important."

"That depends," Ed said, keeping his eyes front. "I don't know what to say to a girl like you. First you jump out of a car with two tough eggs in it. Then you hide in mine. Then you hold me up and want to take ten grand away from me. Then you ask me to promise you something—"

"Please!" she repeated earnestly. "That telegram—"

She stopped, ducked down again. They had turned the corner after Seeley, and were entering the spacious parking grounds outside the dog track. Seeley had slowed up, and was alongside again, and the girl had not ducked down a moment too soon. Whatever she wanted to say would remain unsaid.

The cop motioned to an empty parking spot, and Ed maneuvered into it. Seeley had got off his cycle, and was opening the door of the car almost before Ed had turned off the ignition.

"It's ten to nine, Mister Race," the cop said. "Let's hurry. If Charley Wiener said it was life and death, then it must be serious."

Ed cast a furtive glance into the rear, saw the girl snuggling down. He shrugged. She seemed to know something about Charley's frantic telegram. But she was equally anxious not to be caught. He would have to forego hearing what she had to say.

He left the car, walked arm in arm with Seeley through the gate. Seeley waved to the gateman, and they didn't have to pay any admission. Within, there was a throng of gay, carefree people, bustling about, hurrying to place bets at the mutuel windows, exchanging jests and giving each other tips. A band was playing in the grandstand, and on the track eight grey-hounds were being marched up and down in leash, led by eight brightly uniformed pages. The big, electrically illuminated board out in the middle of the field showed that this was the third race, scheduled for 9:05.

Ed fingered the telegram in his pocket, said worriedly: "How the hell are we going to find Charley Wiener in this crowd? He—"

Seeley gripped his arm, pointed. There, at the rail, just opposite the judge's box, stood Charley Wiener. He was watching the dogs parade and didn't seem to have a care in the world.

Seeley pushed through the gay throng, saying over his shoulder to Ed: "Hell, he doesn't look like he was in a life-and-death jam!"

Ed didn't think so either, but there was no telling from Charley's poker-face. Charley Wiener was a sportsman. He owned a string of bungalows in Rockaway, in New York, and worked like a beaver in the summer, up north. In the winter he came down to Miami and blew in everything he made in the summer on the dogs. He had been training dogs for five years now but had failed to develop a single winner. Every once in a while he would call Ed Race on the 'phone, and excitedly give him a tip. The tip invariably cost Ed money. But Charley was a good fellow, and Ed felt that someday he would bring a winner to the track.

When Ed got through the crowd and reached his side, Charley had his elbows on the rail, his chin cupped in his hands, and was studying the eight greyhounds. Ed tapped him on the shoulder, said:

"Hello, Charley. I got here as quick as I could. Hope I'm in time. You don't look like you're in a jam." Ed was fumbling in his watch pocket as he spoke, and he pulled out a crumpled bill. "I brought the ten grand—got it all in one bill. I hope it squares you."

Charley Wiener took his hand enthusiastically, pumped it up and down. "Hello, Eddie. Haven't seen you for six months. I knew you'd come." He nodded to Seeley. "Hiya, Tom! Want a good dog for this race?"

Seeley grinned, looked puzzled. "What's the trouble, Mr. Wiener?"

Wiener threw him an inquiring glance. "Trouble?"

Seeley stared at him. "You're in a jam, aren't you?"

"Jam? What do you mean?" He let his glance slide from Seeley to Ed. "What are you guys doing—ribbing me?"

Ed said: "Look here, Charley. I brought your ten grand. Your telegram said you had to have it—or else. Well, here it is. If you don't care to talk about it, that's okay with me. Maybe it's something personal. I'm sure Seeley, here, won't let it get any further. The reason he knows about it is because he stopped me on the causeway for speeding, and I had to show him your telegram to get out of it. When he saw it was a matter of life and death with you, he escorted me here. He's—"

ED STOPPED, staring. Charley Wiener had suddenly burst out laughing, uncontrollably. He slapped his knee, slapped Ed on the shoulder, patted Seeley on the back. "Well, I'll be damned! So you thought I was in a jam, and you brought the dough!"

Ed said irritably: "Listen, Charley, it's no joke. Here's your telegram."

He took out the crumpled form, and Wiener seized it, still laughing.

"Gee, I never thought you'd take it that way, Eddie. I guess I didn't figure it would sound like that. I forgot you didn't know Life and Death!"

"What do you mean—I didn't know Life and Death?"

"My dog, Eddie. That's my dog's name!" He opened his racing card, pointed to the entries for the third race. There it was, staring up at Ed:

> Number 8—Life and Death—67 lbs.
> Owner, Charles Wiener

Ed raised his eyes from the card, stared at Seeley, then at Charley Wiener. "Well, you son-of-a-gun! Dragging me out here, and me thinking you were up against a life-and-death jam!"

"Look," Charley said eagerly, pointing to his own telegram. "Life and Death *has* to win. He outclasses every dog in the race. And it's the last chance to bet on him. I'm selling out my stable tonight and going north. My daughter is going to be married.

That's why I sent you this telegram. You've bet ten grand on horses and dogs before. Look—" He pointed to the board out on the field. "— the odds are only one to one, but it's an absolutely sure bet. You lay down that ten grand, and you'll double your money. I've already put every cent I could scrape up on him!"

Ed said: "Charley, I'd like to push your face in. Here you get me all excited, thinking you're in trouble. I race out here from Palm Beach, all hell-bent for leather. I have to get back to Palm Beach by ten-thirty. My number goes on—"

Charley gripped his arm. "Go on, Ed. Lay that ten grand. You can collect and get back to the theater in plenty of time."

Ed shrugged, glanced at Seeley. "What can you do with a guy like that?" he asked hopelessly.

Seeley grinned, dug into his pocket and pulled out two ten-dollar bills, a five and three singles. "Here's twenty-eight bucks I feel like gambling with."

"All right." Ed thrust the ten-thousand-dollar bill into his hand. "Let's all be crazy. Here, you take mine over to the mutuel window too, while you're at it."

Seeley took the bill, and pushed his way through the crowd toward the rear, where the cashiers' cages were located.

Charley Wiener said: "You won't regret this one, Eddie. It's a sure thing. Look at that dog. He can't lose!" He pointed at the greyhounds, which were just being lined up in front of the judge's box, having their muzzles and covers tested to assure that they would not be hampered in running.

Ed appraised each of them in turn with the shrewd eye of an expert. They were all sleek, well-groomed, aching to go. Number eight impressed Ed. The hound's long body and lean flanks spoke of tremendous reserve power. It carried itself well, with the poise of a thoroughbred.

Charley Wiener glowed with pride. "I tell you, Eddie, I got a winner this time. He outclasses the other seven. Number three would walk away with this race if it wasn't for Life and Death. Look—number three's odds are up to five to two. It was even money when the betting started."

Ed was inclined to agree with Charley that Life and Death would walk away with the race. The band stopped playing, and the dogs started marching to the line. The announcer up at the microphone called out:

"You have exactly five minutes to place your bets, ladies and gentlemen. The cashiers at the rear are waiting for you. Don't delay till the last minute, or you may not be able to lay down a bet."

A young man approached Charley and Ed. He was in the neighborhood of twenty-three or twenty-four, fair-haired, with clean-cut features and a high forehead. He was dressed in tan flannel trousers and a tan sport jacket.

CHARLEY WIENER hailed him gaily. "Hi there, Ronny. Want you to meet my best friend—Eddie Race. You know, the guy that shoots-'em-up on the stage. Eddie, this is Ronny Greer, my future son-in-law. He's going to marry Gloria. You've never met Gloria, have you?"

Ed shook hands with Ronny Greer, while Charley went on: "Ronny is a dog owner, too. He owns number three—the hound that would win this race if Life and Death wasn't in it."

Ronny Greer made a face. "You're right. I've never seen you with a winner yet, and you have to go and pick one when I've got my best dog entered! I think I'll go and place a bet on Life and Death myself!"

He left them, and Charley said glowingly: "He's a swell kid, Ronny is. He knows more about dogs than I do. Gloria met him when she was in Europe. When she gets married, I'll sell out all my bungalows in Rockaway, and take Lucie and the twins for a trip around the world."

Ed had met Lucie, Charley's wife, and his other two children, Billy and Stephen. Billy and Stephen were twins, and Ed could never tell them apart. They were only six years old, and they had a lot of fun making Ed guess which was which. He had never met Gloria, because she had been away at a finishing school, and later in Europe.

Seeley came back with Ed's mutuel ticket, and his own. The crowd surged up around them, close to the rail, as the dogs were placed in the starting box. A bugle sounded to indicate that no more bets would be accepted. Everybody grew tense as the dogs waited to be released. About two hundred feet back of the starting box, the mechanical bunny was started, and its white shape flashed under the brilliant incandescent lights as it sped around the inside of the track.

The announcer up in the grandstand called into his microphone in a playful voice: "Heeeere comes the bun-ny!"

And at that moment an almost hysterical voice behind the spot where Ed and Charley and Seeley were standing shouted: "Dad! Dad!"

Charley Wiener swung around, and Ed, following his glance, saw that the girl he had left in the car outside was struggling to get through to them. Her face was flushed, her eyes distended.

Charley Wiener paid no attention to the dogs. He started pushing toward the excited girl. "Gloria!" he shouted. And Ed Race's eyes narrowed. Gloria! This girl that he had seen leap from the big sedan was Charley Wiener's daughter!

He and Seeley pushed after Wiener, came out of the throng just as Charley met his daughter in the cleared space behind the crowd. Gloria threw only a single glance at Ed, then gripped her father's arm.

"Dad! Life and Death isn't going to win! They know about the siren! They're going to sound the siren! They came to the house and took Billy and Stephen and me away, and they said they'd—they'd do things to the twins if I didn't tell them what was wrong with Life and Death. They knew there was some secret about him. So—so I told them. And then they took me along in a car, but I jumped out of it. I—I was afraid to tell the police, because those two men still had Billy and Stephen. What'll we do?"

Charley Wiener seemed dazed. He gazed helplessly at Ed and Seeley.

Ed didn't understand what she was talking about. "What's this about a siren?"

Charley Wiener groaned. "It's Life and Death's only weakness. He was frightened by a siren when he was a pup. Whenever he hears one, he quits. He—"

WIENER STOPPED, his face going gray as there came to them from somewhere outside the track the shrill notes of a siren. Its keen, wailing tone spread over the track, and Ed, glancing out at the dogs which were just rounding the turn for the home stretch, saw number eight, in the lead, falter and swerve.

In a moment the leading dog had flashed over the finish line, and the race was over. Number three had won!

Charley Wiener didn't care, however. He had Gloria by the arm, was questioning her fiercely. "The twins! Where are the twins? To hell with the race. What's happened to Billy and Stephen?"

Gloria was sobbing. "I don't know, Dad. They b-blindfolded us when they took us away. I—I don't know."

The crowd was pushing past their little group now, some making for the mutuel windows to collect on their tickets. On the tote board, electric bulbs spelled:

$2.00 ticket on No. 3 pays—$6.00

Charley Wiener's face was gray. "My God, Eddie," he said, "I don't give a damn about the race. I want those two kids back!"

Ed said: "Come on. Let's get out!"

He made his way toward the exit, followed by Charley, Gloria and Seeley. Seeley caught up with him, took his arm. "This is kidnapping, Mr. Race. I guess I better 'phone in, and report."

Ed nodded. "Get to a 'phone. I'm going to find who sounded that siren outside."

At the gate he said to Charley Wiener, "You wait here with Gloria. I'll be right back. Get hold of the track officials, tell them to locate this here Ronny Greer. His dog won the race by default."

Gloria exclaimed, "But, Mr. Race, Ronny couldn't have had anything to do with it! He wouldn't hurt Billy and Stephen!"

"You may be right," Ed told her glumly, "but it doesn't hurt to investigate."

He left them, passed through the gate and was about to question the attendant, when out of the corner of his eye he caught sight of a figure that looked a little familiar to him, slinking in among the parked cars. He could have sworn it was the stocky man whom he had tangled with back at Biscayne Boulevard.

Ed ducked in between two cars in the next row, bent low, and crept after him. He came out on the other side, and almost bumped into a close-huddled group of four men, with their heads together. It was pretty dark here, but Ed recognized the profile of Ronny Greer.

Greer was saying: "All right, you guys. Here's your dough. Now amscray. We'll leave the twins—"

He stopped as one of the men sensed Ed's presence, raised his head. It was the stocky man, who had just joined the group. His eyes rested on the figure of Ed Race, in the shadow, and he said hoarsely, "Somebody's there!"

At the same time, Ed's hand flashed up to his shoulder holster, came out with a gun. One of the big forty-fives appeared in his right hand as if by magic, and its deep-toned roar sounded a split-second sooner than the stocky man's gun. The stocky man went crashing backward, dead on his feet.

The other three men separated, darting to either side, among the cars. Shots began coming Ed's way from three directions. Ed knelt beside the car, firing methodically at the flashes, with both guns out now. Bullets clanged against the steel of the car against which he rested, and slugs whistled past his head. But Ed's bleak face did not move a muscle there in the darkness as he traded shots. He was thinking of the twins. Suddenly one of the three uttered a shriek, and his body fell forward to the ground. Ed had caught him in the chest, firing at his flash. The other two were in darkness at the edge of the parking lot, and they had the advantage, because the lights of the track were behind Ed. They could see him, but he could not see them.

A BULLET nicked Ed's shoulder, tearing the coat, and burning lightly across his skin. He dropped lower, firing almost from the ground, but unable to see what he was shooting at. And suddenly, aid came to him from an unexpected source. The headlamps of the car he was leaning against abruptly went on, bathing the darkness in the bright glare of their luminance. Ed saw, outlined in their glow, the figures of his two remaining assailants, firing over the hood of the car ahead. One of them was Ronny Greer, the other was the thin man who had been in the sedan with the stocky one. Both blinked in the glare of the headlamps.

Ed couldn't guess who was in the car, who had snapped the lights on, but he took advantage of the opportunity. Both his guns spoke at exactly the same time. Ed didn't have to go over there to look at them; he knew they were dead.

Instead, he turned to the car, wrenched open the door, and looked in. Two tow-headed, tousled kids were in there, looking up at him with laughing eyes. They were both gagged, and their hands tied.

Ed exclaimed: "Billy and Stephen!"

He tore the gags from them, and his fingers worked swiftly untying the ropes that held the little wrists. As soon as the gags were off, they both started to talk together: "Uncle Ed! We saw you shoot! Gee, you can sure shoot!"

Ed asked: "Who turned on the headlights?"

One of the youngsters said proudly, "I did, Uncle Ed! I wanted to see how you shot those bad men, so I turned around in the seat, and reached the lights and turned them on. Gee, it was great!"

There was a rush of feet behind them, and Charley Wiener pushed Ed aside, fell on the twins, hugging and kissing them. Gloria, behind him, was pawing over his shoulder at them.

A crowd had poured out from the track at the sound of the shots, and several uniformed men, with Seeley at their head.

Ed pointed to the dead bodies. "It's all over but the funerals," he told Seeley. "That guy, Greer, was behind it all. He knew there was something phony about Life and Death, so he had those other birds kidnap the twins and Gloria, and force the secret from her. He knew if he could get Life and Death out of the race he could win at big odds."

Gloria looked up at Ed. "It—it was Ronny who was in back of it all?"

Charley Wiener lifted the twins out of the car. "My God, Gloria," he said, "you almost married the guy!"

She buried her face in her hands.

The twins didn't seem to mind. They started climbing up Ed, pulling themselves up by his coat. "Uncle Ed!" they shouted. "See if you can guess: Which is Billy and which is Stephen?"

Ed laughed. "I give up!" He glanced at Seeley, who was looking mournfully at his tote tickets.

"Lookit that," Seeley exclaimed. "Twenty-eight bucks shot!"

Ed said, "How about my ten grand?"

Charley Wiener heaved a sigh. "The race is going to be declared off," he announced. "All bets will be refunded. And I'm quitting the dog races—for good!"

Ed grinned at him. "Without ever having a winner?"

"To hell with it!" said Charley. "I'm going to stick to the bungalow business from now on. It's less of a gamble!"

BAD ACTORS DIE YOUNG!

O N SATURDAY night, Ed Race finished his engagement at the Palm Beach Theater. Sunday afternoon he went up to Daytona Beach to give a benefit performance for the Florida Easter Fund, and it was at Daytona that the telegram from Leon Partages caught him. Partages was the owner of the vaudeville circuit for which Ed worked, and Ed always had a soft spot in his heart for the kindly, genial, old gentleman. Partages generally did the craziest things on the spur of the moment, and it appeared from the telegram that he was now doing one of them:

ED RACE
C/O DAYTONA THEATER DAYTONA FLORIDA
   YOU ARE OPENING IN MIAMI BEACH MONDAY
STOP GO THERE TONIGHT INSTEAD AND BUY A
HORSE NAMED REDTAIL FROM ARTHUR FRINK
ITS PRESENT OWNER STOP THIS HORSE IS A WOW
STOP IT HAS WON FOUR RACES STRAIGHT AND
IT IS ENTERED IN THE FOURTH AT HIALEAH
TOMORROW AGAINST BANG-UP WHICH IS
ANOTHER GOOD HORSE THAT WON THE DERBY
STOP ARTHUR FRINK IS BROKE AND THEY HAVE
ATTACHED HIS SHARE OF THE PURSE IF REDTAIL

WINS STOP HE WILL GLADLY TAKE TWELVE
THOUSAND FOR THE HORSE STOP I HAVE WIRED
YOU THE MONEY AT WESTERN UNION STOP GO
THERE AND PICK UP THE TWELVE THOUSAND
AND SEE FRINK AT MCCORMICK HOTEL STOP
PAY HIM THE MONEY IN ADVANCE STOP HE WILL
GIVE YOU BILL OF SALE DATED TOMORROW AS
REDTAIL IS STILL GOING TO RUN UNDER HIS
COLORS IN TOMORROWS MEET AT HIALEAH
BUT HE NEEDS THE CASH TODAY STOP ALSO
TRY TO KEEP LEE LINTON HIS JOCKEY ON THE
JOB I WANT HIM STOP COMING TO MIAMI WILL
ARRIVE TUESDAY MORNING BY TRAIN AS I GET
SICK EVERY TIME I GO BY PLANE STOP SO LONG
STOP THIS TELEGRAM IS COSTING ME TOO
DAMN MUCH ALREADY STOP THANKS
                                    LEON PARTAGES

Ed Race did a lot of grumbling, but he went to the Western
Union office after the benefit performance, and picked up the
twelve thousand in cash. Then he caught the Florida Special for
Miami, which was two hours late at Daytona.

The rush of tourists for the warm climates was still strong, and
there wasn't a parlor chair available, so Ed got in the day coach.
There were three coaches hitched on behind the engine, and
they were all pretty full. The only seat unoccupied was next to a
blond young lady who was avidly watching the scenery roll by.

Ed raised his hat, inquired politely: "Is this seat taken, miss?"

The young lady had her chin cupped in her left palm, her

elbow resting on the window ledge, and her eyes glued to the view outside. She didn't hear him. Rather than disturb her, Ed slid into the seat quietly, after throwing his hat upon the rack. He had no baggage with him, having checked it through to the Seaview Hotel at Miami Beach. His theater properties were also going through to the Spray Theater on the beach, where he was scheduled to open that evening.

The girl didn't budge, seemed not to be aware of his presence....

Ed glanced around the car. His seat was well toward the rear, and he had a good view of the rest of the occupants. This was a smoker, but there was a goodly percentage of women. Halfway down the car, four men were playing pinochle in a double seat, using a suitcase on their knees for a table. Further down, six men cramped into another double seat, were playing stud poker. Each game had its contingent of kibitzers, and wisecracks were flowing freely. Tobacco smoke and good nature permeated the coach. All these people were coming down for a holiday, getting away from the severe cold of the north. They had left their inhibitions and their false prides behind. Back in the Pullman cars, people would be sitting stiffly, keeping to themselves, conscious of their own importance. Here everybody was having a good time....

ED RACE took out a cigarette, and abruptly became aware that the girl next the window was looking at him. He turned, to find her wide blue eyes fixed on him. He noted, in the quick glance he gave her, that her features seemed a bit pinched, as if from privation, and that there were dark circles under her eyes. But she was pretty. Her skin was soft, smooth, her features small and well modeled.

He smiled, extended the package of cigarettes. "Have a smoke?" he asked.

She hesitated only a fraction of a second, then her face was transformed by a smile, and her long, slim fingers extracted a cigarette.

"Thank you," she murmured.

Ed held the light for her, and he noticed that her hand shook as she held the butt to her lips. She inhaled deeply, let the smoke trickle through her nostrils with a deep sigh of contentment. Her eyes strayed back to the window. "Isn't it beautiful?" she exclaimed. "Oranges are growing on trees, everything green and blooming. And up north—it's hard to believe that only twenty-four hours ago I was freezing in New York!"

Ed appraised her keenly. She was wearing a cheap, tweed coat, unbuttoned to reveal a tan sweater and skirt underneath. Her hat was up on the rack, and her glorious, bobbed hair seemed to make the tawdriness of her clothes negligible.

"This your first trip south?" Ed asked her sympathetically.

She nodded. "I've heard so much of Florida. But it's better than one can imagine!"

She was smoking the cigarette fast, gulping the smoke as if her lungs were starved for it. "You—you come down often?"

"Every year," Ed told her. "It gets in your blood."

She became wistful. "This is my first time—and I'm afraid it's the last."

"Vacation?"

She shook her head. "I haven't worked for two years. I guess I'll have to start again now, though."

Ed followed her glance down to her left hand, where there was a thin, white gold, wedding band, but no engagement ring. He hadn't noticed it before, because she'd been resting her chin on that hand. It came to him as a distinct shock that this frail, china fragile young thing should be a married woman. Two years, hmm! She couldn't have been more than eighteen then, when she was married!

Just then, a colored porter in a white coat came into the car with a tray of sandwiches and a pitcher of coffee. Coach passengers generally didn't patronize the expensive dining cars, so they sold sandwiches and coffee at intervals.

Ed had eaten in Daytona, but he looked at the girl's pinched face, said: "How about a snack? It'll be more than three hours before we hit Miami—"

He stopped at sight of the sudden agony in her face. She was biting her lip. "N-no, thank you. I—"

She grew silent, and Ed saw that her little hands were clenched in her lap. The cigarette she was holding was being crushed.

"Look here," Ed exclaimed impulsively. "You're hungry!"

She closed her eyes. "No, no. Really I'm not!"

Ed paid no attention to her feeble protest, but motioned to the porter. "Three ham sandwiches, and two cups of that mud," he ordered. He paid sixty-five cents, took the paper cups of coffee, and handed one to the girl. There was no more resistance in her. She accepted it, as well as the two sandwiches he placed on her lap. Though he was not hungry himself, Ed ate the third sandwich, watching the girl wolf down her food. He even thought he saw color coming into her cheeks as she ate.

When she was finished, she turned to him impulsively, said: "That's the first thing I've eaten since I left New York. I—I had no money with me."

Ed raised his eyebrows. "It's a long trip to take without any money. Can I—?"

"No—no, thank you. You've been kind enough. I'll be—all right when I get to Miami. And I must pay you back for this. Won't you please tell me where I can send you some money?"

"That's an insult," Ed told her. "I'll be more than glad to see you in Miami—if you'll promise not to try to be absurd. If you'd care to have dinner with me some time—"

HE WAS carefully refraining from asking her for any explanation of why a girl should take a fourteen hundred mile trip without enough money in her purse to buy a sandwich. If she didn't want to explain, that was all right with him. He tore a thin strip from the margin of his timetable, wrote his name on it, and the address of the Spray Theater. He handed it to her. "I hope you'll look me up."

She took the slip of paper, glanced down at it, and suddenly her face went paper white. She uttered a little gasp, and immediately began to cough as if she were trying desperately to cover up the sudden confusion that had assailed her. Ed asked her, puzzled: "What's the trouble? Does my name mean anything to you?"

"Why no, of course not. I mean, yes, I've heard of you. I—I really didn't think a celebrity like you would be traveling in a day coach. You're the man who juggles forty-five caliber guns on the vaudeville stage aren't you? You do acrobatics, and juggle guns at the same time, and shot out the flames of a row of candles while you do somersaults? I've seen you—at the Clyde Theater in New York. I think your act is marvelous!"

She was talking very fast, as if she were afraid of stopping.

Ed nodded thoughtfully. "That's right," he said. "I'm billed as The Masked Marksman."

She smiled. "The Man Who Can Make Guns Talk. I've seen that line on all the billboards. And they say you always carry two of your guns with you in twin shoulder holsters. Is that true?"

Ed nodded again. He was thinking very fast. Not one person in ten thousand knew that Ed Race was the Masked Marksman. He always appeared on the stage with a mask. How did this girl, meeting him apparently by chance on the train, know his identity? If he was tempted to quiz her on that point, he lost the opportunity, for at that moment a small, scrawny man with a bald head got up from the poker game down front, and came walking up the aisle disconsolately. He was a dapper individual, neat looking in spite of the obvious fact that he must have been sitting up in the day coach overnight. His ears were small, stuck close in to his skull, and his eyes were also small and very close together over a thin, almost midget nose. His mouth was drawn down at the corners, and he looked as if he had just learned of the loss of his dearest relative.

Ed saw him, and grinned, calling out: "Hello there, Mac!"

The man raised his eyes from the floor, and suddenly let out a whoop of joy at sight of Ed. "Ye gods and little fishes!" he shouted, startling everybody in the car. He raced up to the seat, seized Ed's hand and pumped it up and down with a vigor and strength unsuspected in such a little man. "If it ain't Eddie Race in person! God's gift to Danny McGlone in his hour of desperation! Eddie, you're a lifesaver! Lend me fifty, will you? Those buzzards cleaned me out in stud poker, and I'm just beginning to feel lucky!"

Ed grinned, dug into his pocket, and peeled a fifty dollar bill off a sizable roll. "How much did you drop, Mac?" Ed asked him.

"Two and a half C's, Eddie—all the dough I owned. And I

was all set to make a killing with it down at Hialeah tomorrow. I got to get my dough back."

Ed Race glanced at the girl, said: "Mr. McGlone, I want to you to meet Miss—er—"

He waited, and she had to supply the name: "Mrs. Linton," she said, after a moment's hesitation.

McGlone, eager to get back to the game, started to say hastily: "Pleased to meetcha—" and then stopped short, his eyes narrowing. "Linton? Did you say Linton? You any relation to Lee Linton, the jockey?"

Her face was flushed a bit. "Yes. I'm his wife."

McGlone murmured: "Oh, yeah? I see." He was silent a minute, then: "Well, Eddie, I got to get back in the game. Look me up at the Hotel Tropical. I'll have the fifty for you any time after the races tomorrow."

HE LEFT them, and Ed turned to the girl, found her looking at him queerly. Ed had sensed something peculiar about the way McGlone reacted upon learning her name. To put her at her ease again, he tried to make light conversation.

"You know, McGlone is probably the most unscrupulous person I know. He used to be a handicapper at Saratoga, but he was barred from the track. And yet, he has his good points. For instance, I'll get that fifty back, just as sure as the sun will rise in Miami tomorrow."

She didn't seem interested. She was still regarding, with a strange, speculative look, the unfinished sandwich in one hand, the paper cup of coffee in the other. She finished eating in silence. The train was racing through a kaleidoscope of glowing, sun warmed country. The trainman came through, announced: "The next stop will be West Palm Beach."

She crumpled the empty paper cup, put the waxed paper from her sandwiches carefully into it, and crushed the whole thing. Ed did the same with his, took the cup from her and went to the rear, deposited both in the waste receptacle under the water-cooler. When he came back, she had finished powdering her nose. She said casually: "That was an awful lot of money you took out just now, when you gave that man the fifty dollars."

Ed nodded. "There's twelve thousand dollars in that roll." He watched her out of the corner of his eye. "I'm going to buy a horse for a friend of mine."

She didn't answer. The train began to slow down for the West Palm Beach station. Then she said vivaciously: "Is it really true that you carry two guns with you?"

He laughed. "I certainly do."

"W-would you let me see one of them?"

Ed drew the heavy forty-five from his left holster, handed it to her, butt first. She took it, hefted it in her hand.

"You want to be careful of it," Ed told her. "It has a hair trig-ger."

She seemed to be tensing herself for something. The train was pulling into the station. Suddenly she turned, poked the muzzle of the gun into Ed's side. Her lips were trembling, and there was a frantic light in her eyes. "Give me that money in your pocket!" she commanded.

Ed looked down at the gun, saw that it was shaking in her hand. He sighed, said: "I've heard of this sort of thing being pulled by hitchhikers, but not in a train. You have your nerve with you!"

"It's not nerve," she said tightly. "It's desperation. I'll shoot if you don't give me that money before we stop."

Ed slowly put his hand in his pocket, took out the thick roll.

"You can take off two hundred dollars for your expenses," she said.

Ed grinned sardonically. "Very considerate of you," he murmured, and peeled off two bills, handed her the rest. "Would you care for my wrist watch, too? It's a very fine watch. Fourteen carat gold, eighteen jewel—"

She broke in. "Whatever you think of me, I deserve it—repaying your kindness this way. But believe me, I'm at the end of my rope. I'm so desperate that neither your life nor mine can stand in the way!"

Ed said nothing, but watched her. The train had stopped. "Give me your other gun!" she ordered.

He took it out, handed it to her, butt first, as he had done with the other one. She placed it under her coat, and stood up, still keeping him covered. People were moving down the aisle, getting off, and no one paid them any attention. She held the gun with which she covered him close in the folds of her coat.

Ed asked her curiously: "How are you going to get off the train? You know I could come after you the minute you turn your back. You surely aren't going to shoot at me through all that crowd of innocent people?"

"You're coming with me!" she told him. "Get up and walk to

the front of the car. Keep right in front of me, and don't try to run. If you do, I swear I'll shoot!"

SHE MOVED out into the aisle, and Ed got up, smiling faintly. He made his way along the aisle, with the girl close behind him. When he passed the seat where the poker game was going on, McGlone looked up at him with a long face. "Hiya, Ed? The fifty's almost gone. I can't get a break with these here vultures. Stick around a couple of minutes. Maybe you'll bring me luck."

Ed felt something hard poked against the small of his back, and he said pleasantly to McGlone: "Sorry, Mac. If I don't get out in the fresh air, I'll die. It's too damn stuffy in here."

He passed on into the vestibule, stepped down onto the station platform. He could have twisted to one side there, and gotten out of range of the girls gun, but he didn't. He waited very docilely for her to come down after him. Her capacious tweed coat hid the gun effectually. She stepped up to him, her eyes burning feverishly out of a flushed face. "Go through the station," she ordered, "and hail a cab."

The hot sun was pouring down on the station. The train would stop here for ten minutes, and hundreds of passengers were out on the platform, enjoying their first whiff of Florida air.

Ed said: "Lady, I want to compliment you. You're a first-class bandit and kidnaper. You couldn't get rid of me now, if you wanted to. I've got to stick with you and see what your play is going to be."

He pushed through the station to the curb, and motioned to

a cab. They got into it, and the girl said: "Drive us to the nearest bank."

Ed started to chuckle, but immediately stopped, studying her in a puzzled way.

She sat in the corner of the car, half facing Ed, with the gun wrapped in her coat. She was breathing hard, almost panting. Ed could see that the nervous strain under which she was laboring was terrific. She forced herself to calmness, and said: "When we get to the bank, were going inside, and you will open an account in your own name, and deposit this twelve thousand dollars. I'll be standing right behind you, and if you should try to spoil it in any way, I'll shoot you!"

Ed asked her: "You mean that you've done all this, just to get me to deposit the money in a bank?"

She nodded.

"Lady," he said, "you're full of surprises. Can it be that you're not a bandit at all, but just a high-powered salesman for a bank?"

She didn't answer, just sat there looking at him.

From the direction of the station they heard the departing whistle of the Florida Special. Ed said: "There go our hats!"

The cab stopped, and the driver announced: "Here it is, lady. You wanted the bank, didn't you?"

Ed opened the door, held it for her. She got out awkwardly, because she was still trying to keep him covered. She started to say: "Pay the driv—" but stopped short, her face paling, as her eyes lighted on the bank. She gasped: "Why! It—it's closed!"

Ed grinned. "Most banks are closed on Sunday. It's an old banking custom."

She swung on the cab driver. "Why didn't you tell me?"

The driver shrugged, winked at Ed. "It wasn't none of my business, lady. You said you wanted to go to the bank, so I brung you. How did I know you had the days of the week mixed? You might of just wanted to show this here gentleman the arkyte-chure. It's a swell looking building, ain't it?"

She was wavering now, full of indecision. Ed took out some change, paid off the cabby. "Beat it," he said.

The driver pocketed his fare and the tip. "You ain't sore, are you, mister? Why don't you let me take you back to the station or someplace? It's pretty hot, walkin'—"

"That's all right, my friend," Ed told him. "We'll wait here for the bank to open."

The driver stared, and then shrugged. "Okey doke by me, mister. I'll come back for you Monday morning."

He threw the car in gear, and pulled away. Ed turned to the girl. "Well, Miss Bandit, where to now? You've still got the gun—"

HE WAS interrupted by a hoarse shout. A second taxicab had pulled in at the curb, and Dan McGlone erupted from within it. His face was red with excitement, and he had a small, gun-metal automatic in his hand. He hurled himself across the sidewalk, and poked the automatic into the girls side.

"Drop that gun!" he snapped at her. "Drop it quick!"

Startled, the girl let the heavy revolver fall from the fold of her coat. It banged on the sidewalk, but did not explode. McGlone swung on Ed. "I seen that something was phony, when you was walking down the aisle in the car. So I looked out the window, and seen you two get in the cab. In my life I have known many a guy to be taken for a ride, and if this wasn't the goods, I'd of eaten my shirt. I could of sworn that she was holding a gun on you. So I got out of the train and followed. And here we are!"

He spoke triumphantly, like one who has accomplished a deed of rare heroism.

Ed Race said sourly: "Thanks, Mac. Your intentions were fine. But you didn't have to worry." He stooped and picked up the revolver, broke it, exhibited an empty chamber. "This revolver was unloaded. I carry the cartridges in my pocket, because my guns have hair triggers!"

McGlone swore disgustedly, and put his automatic away. His cabby came over hesitantly, said: "Would yoh mind payin' yoh fare, mistah?" He glanced timidly at the big revolver that Ed still held. "Not that I insist, of co'se, but I have a wife an' foah kids at home, and I could use the money—"

McGlone shifted uneasily from one foot to another, looked sheepishly at Ed. "Say, Eddie—could you maybe fix this guy up? I—I happen to be flat again—"

Ed raised his eyebrows, took out some more change, and paid the man. When the driver had gone, Ed asked McGlone: "What happened to the fifty, Mac?"

McGlone lowered his eyes. "I—er—aw, hell! Those buzzards were too good for me. I'm clean again!"

Ed grinned. "The wisest guy is always a sucker for somebody else's game, Mac. Take you for instance—you take 'em over at the tracks, and drop it all in poker. You—say—!"

The girl had been standing quietly. Now she had turned

suddenly and had started to run at breakneck speed away from them, toward the main highway, a block away.

McGlone exclaimed: "Hell, what a wildcat!" and started after her. But Ed caught his arm, held him back. "Take it easy, Mac. It's my money she has. If I want her, I'll go after her."

They watched her run, with the coat flapping awkwardly behind her. On the way, something fluttered out of her pocket, unnoticed by her, and dropped to the sidewalk. She kept on without stopping. They saw her reach the highway, look back, and raise a thumb toward a passing car. It sped past her without stopping, but a second one, right behind it, a beautiful, maroon sedan with six wire wheels, ground to a stop, and they saw her get into it, saw the car pull away toward the south....

Ed sighed. "That's that!"

McGlone asked: "Has she got your dough?"

"She has. Twelve thousand dollars."

McGlone whistled. "You crazy, Eddie? You let her get away!"

"Well, not exactly. I intend to follow her. I want to see where she goes and what she does when she gets to Miami. There's something damn queer in the wind—"

"But how the hell you gonna follow her? That cars traveling like—"

"She left me two hundred dollars, Mac. Very kind hearted of her." Ed walked him down the street, picked up the red-white-and-blue bordered envelope which had fluttered from the girl's pocket. "We'll locate the airport and hire a plane. It's only sixty miles to Miami. We should be there in a half hour. We'll watch for that maroon sedan."

McGlone shrugged. "You're the boss, Eddie, I haven't got a sou, so I'll string along with you. But I think you're nuts just the same. First you let a dizzy dame hold you up with an empty gun, and then you let her get away with twelve grand, when you could have grabbed her as easy as you could say Jack Robinson!" ED WASN'T listening. He was keeping an eye out for a cab, and at the same time he was loading his revolver from a box of cartridges he had taken from his pocket.

By the time he got the gun loaded, a cab hove into sight. It was the same driver who had brought Ed and the girl to the bank, and he leaned out, grinned. "I got an idea you might get hungry, waitin' for the bank to open, mister, so I figured I'd come around and take you to a restaurant."

"Very thoughtful of you," Ed told him. "I'll tell you what you do—drive us to the airport—and make it snappy!"

The driver looked at McGlone, asked Ed: "Where's the lady, mister?"

Ed climbed in the cab, scowled at the driver. "She's still looking for a bank. Get going!"

On the way to the airport, Ed kept fingering the envelope he had picked up, turning it over and over in his hands. It was an airmail letter, with the postage canceled, and it had evidently been received, opened and read. It was addressed to Mrs. Mary Linton, Hotel Channing, New York City. The return address was: Lee Linton, McCormick Hotel, Miami, Florida.

McGlone, who had grown morosely silent, suddenly started to talk: "Look, Eddie, I'm dead broke now, but you see how much you can hold on to out of that two hundred the dame left you. The plane fares shouldn't be more than fifty bucks for the both of us. If you have a hundred and a half left, I know how I can make us a couple of G's at the track tomorrow."

Absently, Ed said: "Yes? How?"

"It's a sure bet, Eddie," McGlone told him eagerly. "You keep this to yourself, now. I got connections with a betting syndicate in New York, an' they're throwing the works on *Bang-Up* in the fourth at Hialeah tomorrow. It should pay about twenty to one. And this is no hooey, Eddie. You know I get 'em straight."

Ed sat up. *"Bang-Up?* Isn't that the race where *Redtail* is running?"

"That's right, Eddie. But *Redtail* won't win. Artie Frink owns her, and he's up against it. He's talked his jockey, Lee Linton, into throwing the race. That's why I was sort of stunned when you introduced me to Linton's wife back there on the train. But see, Eddie, that makes *Bang-Up* a sure winner. We put a hundred and a half on her on the nose—"

"How do you know that Linton is going to throw the race?" Ed asked it calmly, but he was queerly cold. He was thinking of the desperate eyes of Mary Linton.

"How do I know? Because Frink wired the syndicate in code. He wanted to borrow ten grand to bet against himself on *Bang-Up,* and he had to tell them all about it. They would only give him two grand. They wired it to him. But the syndicate is betting about a hundred grand all over the country with the different handbooks. They're not placing it at the track, so as not to pull the odds down."

"I see," Ed said softly. He understood now why Frink wanted

the twelve thousand in advance. He wanted it to bet on *Bang-Up*. At twenty to one, he could clean up a quarter of a million dollars.

Ed said softly: "Hell, I've got to read this!" He pulled the letter out of the opened airmail envelope. There were two things in it—a letter and a telegram. The letter read as follows:

Mary Dear,

I'm going to throw that race for Frink. I'm afraid of what they'll do to both of us if I refuse. I'm broke, and I haven't been able to send you any money for a month. And Frink's gang here will kill me if I don't play ball with them, and then where will you be, without a nickel of insurance? Frink and his crowd are desperate enough to commit murder—or worse. And they've promised me five thousand dollars out of the profits. Mary, I know how you feel about it, but it's better to do this thing than to be dead. See if you can dig up enough for coach fare to come down here. Yours,

Lee.

The telegram was addressed to Mrs. Mary Linton on board the Florida Special at Jacksonville:

PARTAGES BUYING HORSE FOR TWELVE THOUSAND STOP PAYING IN ADVANCE STOP FRINK USING THE MONEY TO BET ON RACE STOP PARTAGES SENDING MONEY BY ED RACE WHO IS THE MASKED MARKSMAN STOP RACE WILL BOARD YOUR TRAIN AT DAYTONA STOP KEEP OUT OF HIS WAY SO HE WONT RECOGNIZE YOU LATER

STOP HE WILL PROBABLY BE IN PULLMAN SO YOU
WONT MEET HIM STOP SORRY DEAR I GOT YOUR
WIRE BUT I CANT BACK OUT NOW STOP IT WILL
ALL COME OUT ALL RIGHT STOP WHEN YOU
ARRIVE COME DIRECTLY TO THE MCCORMICK.

LEE

Ed was silent for a long time after he read those two messages.
McGlone ventured: "Whatsamatter, Eddie? You look like you
seen a ghost!"

"Yes," Ed said somberly. "A very disgusting ghost."

The driver swung the cab in a wide circle into the graveled
driveway of the airport. "Here you are, mister. When you see the
lady, give her my regards."

EXACTLY THIRTY-FIVE minutes later, Ed and
McGlone landed at the International Airport in Miami. And
nine minutes after that they were at the desk of the McCormick Hotel, on the Bay Front. "Mr. Race to see Mr. Frink," Ed
told the clerk.

The clerk 'phoned up, then said: "You can go right up, Mr.
Race. Mr. Frink is expecting you. Room 307."

Ed and McGlone went up in the elevator. The door of 307
was open, and Frink was waiting for them. He was a squat,
bullet-headed man, with very thin eyebrows and a wisp of a
mustache. His reputation as a sportsman was not of the best,
but he was tolerated on the tracks because his family had been
breeders for generations back. He greeted Ed cordially, but when
he caught sight of McGlone he frowned.

McGlone greeted him familiarly. "Hello there, Frinky old

boy! I'm sitting in on this here game. The boys back in N.Y. tipped me off all about it. So you don't have to worry about me."

Frink admitted them, and nodded to a slim, sandy haired young fellow who was sitting in an easy chair sipping a highball, "Mr. Race and Mr. McGlone, I want you to meet my jockey, Lee Linton."

Lee Linton was slight of build, and there was a sort of innate fineness in his face that made it hard to believe he could have been intimidated into throwing a race. At the same time, Ed could easily see how he had been forced to agree, for there were three other men in the room, whom Frink pointedly omitted to introduce. They were all sitting around, drinking highballs, and Ed had never seen a tougher collection outside of the Tombs.

Frink was impatient to get down to business. "I was just having a little—ah—conference with these—er—business associates of mine. But they don't mind waiting, I'm sure."

The three of them grinned. One, a burly chap with a shiny set of false teeth, waved his glass. "Sure, Mr. Frink. Go right ahead. We're comfortable. Don't mind us." Then, after a short pause: "You didn't introduce us to your friends, boss."

Frink grimaced. "This is—er—Jake," indicating the one with the new teeth, "this is Nick, and this is Manny. Mr. Race and Mr. McGlone."

Ed smiled at all three of them disarmingly. Jake grinned, waved his glass negligently; Nick bobbed his head, and Manny got up, bowed mockingly. Jake said: "We're sure pleased to meet-cha, Mister Race an' Mister McGlone."

Lee Linton suddenly put his glass down, stood up determinedly. "Look here, Mr. Race," he began, "You represent Mr. Partages, and I'm sure that if your principal knew how his twelve thousand dollars was to be used—"

He stopped short, for Jake had arisen, moving swiftly for such a bulky man, and taken a position right behind Linton, very close to him. He had his hand in his pocket, and the picket was very close to the jockeys back. He said with deceptive mildness: "You ain't got no call to annoy Mr. Race, now, Lee. Don't you see he wants to get done with this business?"

Linton gulped, looked desperately around the room, and sat down without saying anything further. There was a slight tension in the room which McGlone broke by saying: "Geez, I'm thirsty?"

Jake laughed, went to a decanter on the sideboard, and poured whiskey into a tall glass, then seltzer. He started to fill another one, but Ed said: "None for me, thank you."

Jake raised his eyebrows, handed the glass to McGlone.

Frink stirred impatiently, said to Ed Race: "Now, to get down to business. You—ah—have the money with you, Mr. Race? Twelve thousand dollars, I believe, was the sum that Partages and I agreed on over the 'phone. I have the bill of sale ready here, dated tomorrow. The understanding is that I get the cash now, and you take possession of *Redtail* tomorrow after the fourth race—"

Ed interrupted him. "Unfortunately, Mr. Frink, I haven't got the money!"

There was a stunned silence in the room. Frink repeated dully: "You—haven't got the money?"

Ed shook his head. "I—er—was relieved of it. Perhaps a check—?"

"Hell!" Jake growled. "A checks no good—unless we can cash it. They don't take nothing but U.S. currency at the track—"
HE STOPPED, as if he had said too much, but he was saved embarrassment by the abrupt ringing of the telephone. Frink answered it. He listened a second, exclaimed: "What? His wife? Wait a minute!"

He covered the mouthpiece with his hand, said hoarsely: "It's your wife, Linton. What's she doing here?"

Linton answered defiantly: "I told her to come down. If I'm going to do that for you, I want Mary near me—"

Jake laughed harshly. "Sure, sure. That's all right. Tell her to wait downstairs a few minutes."

Frink nodded, spoke into the 'phone again: "Tell her to wait. We'll be through—" he stopped, listened to the clerk again, then: "She is? Didn't I tell you to have her wait? No, I didn't say send her up, you fool, I said for her to wait. She's in the elevator? Well, okay!"

He slammed the receiver down, glowered at Linton. "The clerk misunderstood me. She's on her way up!"

Jake and his two companions were plainly nonplussed. There was a half glad light in Linton's eyes. Frink tugged at his lower lips, glancing from Ed to McGlone. "You'll pardon me, Mr. Race," he said, "but for certain personal reasons, I do not care that Mrs. Linton should be here while we straighten this matter out. Would you be good enough to go into the adjoining bedroom while we talk to her? I assure you it will only take—"

"That's all right," Ed told him heartily. "Glad to oblige. Sure. Just rap on the door when you're through."

He propelled McGlone by the elbow into the next room, closed the door behind them. They were in the bedroom of the two room suite, and they could hear distinctly every sound that was made in the next room. Florida hotels are far from sound-proof. Some of them have been built in as little as six or seven weeks.

There was the sound of a tap on the door of the sitting room, and then they beard Mary Linton's voice. "Lee! Dearest! You mustn't do it!"

"Mary! S-sh! Don't talk so loud. It's too late now. I told you in the telegram. I can't back out."

"But you must back out. Mr. Frink! Please don't make Lee do a thing like this!"

"I'm sorry, Mrs. Linton," came Frink's suave voice. "Every-thing's arranged. Lee should never have told you about it in the first place. Now he must go through with it—eh, Jake?"

Ed looked at McGlone, as Jake boomed in the next room: "I hope to tell you, lady. He goes through with it—or else!"

"Well then," Mary's voice, defiantly, "I tell you that you won't profit by it. You've got to have the twelve thousand dollars from Partages to bet against yourselves; well, you won't get it! I took the money from Mr. Race, on the train. I'll give it back to him tomorrow—after the fourth race!"

Ed thrilled at the triumphant note in the girl's voice. Even through the closed door, he could sense the throbbing note of defiance.

Frink's voice came to them now, venomous and repressed. "You didn't do anything of the kind. Race is too keen a man to let *you* take his money away—"

"You think so? Well, here it is. I've got it all. I'm going to keep it—till tomorrow!"

Ed glanced at McGlone and groaned: "The little fool! She's just begging for trouble!"

McGlone said, exhibiting remarkable knowledge of human nature: "I think she *wants* trouble, Eddie. She wants to wake up that husband of hers—"

Mary Linton's hysterical voice came to them suddenly: "Stand back. Keep away from me! Don't you try to take this money. I've got a gun here!"

McGlone gripped Ed's sleeve, whispered hoarsely: "My God, Eddie! It's your empty gun!"

Another voice was raised now—Lee Linton's. There was a new note in it. "Damn you, you get your hands off my wife! *Look out!*"

There was the sound of a thudding blow, a falling body, a muted scream.

Ed said to McGlone: "Enter—us!" He pushed open the door, barged in....

MARY LINTON was backed against the wall, her eyes wide with terror. Lee Linton lay at her feet, groaning, with a split lip. Frink stood a little to the left, holding an automatic, while Jake, Nick and Manny, each with a gun, were crowding Mary Linton, who clutched Ed's thick wad of bills in her left hand, and Ed's heavy revolver in her right. At the sound of the opening door they all turned.

Ed said deprecatingly: "Gentlemen! Gentlemen! I'm surprised!"

Jake scowled. "You stay outta this, Race. This don't concern you!"

"On the contrary," Ed said mildly, "it concerns me very much. That money happens to be mine. Why fight over it?"

"That money," said Frink, stepping forward, with the automatic in his hand, "is to be paid to me. Therefore I am interested in getting it."

"I'm sorry, Frink," Ed said coldly, "but after hearing what has been going on, I've decided that Mr. Partages would rather not do business with you. I withdraw the offer to purchase *Redtail.*" He looked across at the girl. "If you'd told me all this on the train, it would have saved a lot of trouble."

She shook her head. "You don't understand. Mr. Race. I *had* to see how Lee would act." There was a glow in her eyes as she glanced down at her husband, struggling to his feet. "And I'm—glad!"

Frink snarled: "Take 'em, boys. That money stays here!"

He stepped back, covered Ed with the automatic. Jake exclaimed: "Yeah!" and stepped forward toward the girl. Linton was on his feet again now, and he drove a weak blow at Jake, who parried it, brought up a terrific uppercut that drove Linton off his feet back against the wall. At the same time, Mary Linton cried out, raised the revolver, and pulled the trigger, aiming it at Jake. The hammer clicked on an empty chamber, and Jake, who had cringed away, uttered a yell and ran at her, with Manny and Nick coming in from either side.

Ed said: "Sorry, Frink," and kicked him in the shins, hard.

Frink yelled, dropped his gun hand for an instant, and Ed's hand flashed in and out from his shoulder holster with the same eye defying speed that had made him a headliner on the vaudeville stage, came out with the loaded revolver. Manny and Nick saw him, and swung their guns toward Ed. Ed sidestepped, slipped behind Frink, gripped him by the collar so he couldn't duck away, and fired twice. Nick and Manny were hurled back against the far wall as if they had been struck by huge catapults. A forty-five slug in the chest will do that to you. Frink squirmed, struggled, but Ed held him fast.

Jake had reached Mary Linton, seized her by the arm, and was swinging her around to make a shield of her just as Ed had done with Frink. Jake fired once, and Frink jerked, moaned, and fell limp. His moan was drowned by the third thunderous explosion of Ed's heavy revolver. Ed's slug caught Jake between the eyes, and the big man was dead before he hit the floor.

Ed let Frink drop, and the racing owner slumped, like a sack, at Ed's feet. Jake's shot had killed him.

Mary Linton was stooping beside her husband, cradling his bleeding head against her breast. "Lee! I knew you'd come through! I knew you weren't yellow!" The wad of money was lying on the floor now, scattered, forgotten.

Ed Race looked around the room for McGlone, couldn't find him, and looked in the bedroom. "Come out of there, Mac!" he called. "It's all over!"

McGlone crawled out from under the bed, dusted himself off. "It ain't that I was scared, Eddie," he said, "but a lady once told me I was born to be hung. And I hate to disappoint her."

Ed went back into the sitting room, and opened the door to the corridor. There was a crowd of frightened people out there, and a couple of bellhops. "You can tell the cops it's all right to come up now," Ed told one of the bellhops.

"W-what happened, mister?"

"Exterminators were here," Ed told him shortly, and turned back.

Mary Linton was supporting Lee, who had gotten to his feet. Linton looked at Ed, said: "I guess I was pretty yellow for a while, Mr. Race. But who could stay yellow with a wife like Mary? Maybe I've got no job, but I've still got her!"

ED SMILED, went to the table and picked up the bill of sale which Frink had already signed. "You still have a job, too, Linton. *Redtail* belongs to Leon Partages now, and you're going to race her for him. I know you'll ride a good race!"

Mary Linton's eyes were wet. She left her husband, stumbled over to Ed, stood on tiptoe, and kissed him on the lips. "We— we'd do *anything* for you—Lee and I!"

Ed grinned. "You can name the first one for me!"

He turned, frowning, to find McGlone plucking at his sleeve. "Geez, Eddie," McGlone said, "you'll have to lend me another fifty to get back to New York. I don't know how to make money on *straight* races!"

MURDER ON THE PROGRAMME

ED RACE stood in front of a one-armed bandit, and kept feeding nickels into it.

Since the supreme court of the State of Florida had declared the slot machines legal, every store in Miami and Miami Beach had at least two of the "one-armed bandits" as the newspapers termed them. Some stores had five and six of them. There were nickel machines, dime machines, and quarter machines. Some of the swankier spots on the Beach even had half-dollar ones. The jackpots in all of them appeared chockfull of coins. You inserted your coin, pulled the handle, and the three drums began to spin. On the drums were colorful pictures of various fruits. If the drums came to rest after their spin, showing the proper combinations of fruits, the machine would click, tinkle, and a number of coins would come clattering out.

Two bunches of cherries paid three nickels; two cherries and a lemon paid five nickels; three oranges paid ten; three plums paid fourteen; three bells paid twenty; and if you were lucky enough to hit three medals, the jackpot opened up, and you took the whole kitty.

Everybody in Miami was pouring nickels, dimes and quarters into the machines. They were geared to pay out about eight percent of their intake, and the operators were making from a hundred to five hundred dollars per week on each machine.

Figuring that there were about three thousand machines in the Greater Miami area, it can readily be seen that the slot-machine business had become the leading industry of Florida.

Ed Race knew it was a sucker's game, but kept putting nickels into the slot because it was only ten thirty, and he had finished his act at the Floridian Theatre, and he wasn't sleepy, and he had nothing better to do between now and the time his train left for Tampa in the morning. He had wandered into the Washington Drug Store, on Washington Avenue, had a cup of coffee and a sandwich, had given the cashier a dollar bill, and had asked for his change in nickels.

There was a crowd of perhaps twenty or twenty-five people at the row of machines. Some were playing, some were waiting for their turn, and others were just getting a vicarious thrill out of seeing other people pull the handles. Ed had started with sixteen nickels. He was down to his last two, and nothing had come out. He put the next to the last one in, pulled the handle, and frowned when he saw a lemon show on the first of the three drums. A man in back of him said sympathetically: "That's done, brother. You can't win with a lemon!"

Ed grunted, started to put the last nickel in, when he felt a timid clutch at his sleeve. He looked down to see a young woman of perhaps nineteen or twenty. She was blue-eyed, pretty, in an innocent sort of way. She was wearing a pair of shorts and one of those tight-fitting bodice brassieres which constitute the entire clothing of the female portion of the population of Miami Beach during the day. This was night time, though, and her attire seemed a bit out of place. Her face was even prettier than

it might ordinarily have been, for she appeared to be flushed—whether it was sunburn, paint, or embarrassed confusion, Ed Race couldn't tell at the moment.

The girl was pulling at his sleeve and saying, "W-would you let me put that nickel in for you? I—feel lucky tonight."

Ed grinned broadly, said: "Sure, sister. Give it a try." He handed her the nickel, pushed aside, and watched her reach up to the slot, insert the coin, and pull the handle. He kept his eyes on her rather than on the machine, as she watched the drums breathlessly, one hand pressed hard at her throat. Her lips were moving as if she was praying....

THE DRUMS came to rest, and she cried, "It hit!" Ed glanced

at them; saw that they had settled on three bells. The machine clanged inside, and coins rattled out of it. She turned to him eagerly, eyes shining. "I told you! It paid twenty!"

"Sister," Ed told her, "you're good!" He scooped the coins out, counted them. There were twenty. He took her arm, pushed a way out of the crowd for both of them, and counted out ten nickels, and handed them to her. "Fifty-fifty. You earned it!"

She hesitated, then took them, flashed him a grateful glance, then went over to the cashier's desk. Ed watched her, puzzled, as she exchanged the ten nickels for two quarters, then made her way back to the machines. As she passed him, Ed said: "You going to play the quarter machine?"

She nodded. "Yes. I—I feel I'm going to win!"

Ed followed her to the machine. "I think you're goofy, sister, but I hope you're right!"

The two quarter machines weren't getting as much of a play as the dime and nickel ones, and she didn't have to wait. With Ed right behind her, she reached up, inserted her quarter, and pulled the handle. As the drums whirled, Ed leaned closer to her, and distinctly heard her whisper: "I've *got* to win! Please God, make me win!" Her bare shoulders and back were tanned, smooth. There was a sweet perfume in her hair, which came up to just below Ed's chin. He could look over her head, could see the drums stop—with the pictures of three bells showing! Twenty quarters clanked out of the machine, and the girl scooped them up with trembling hands, stacked them in her palm.

She turned around, and Ed could see that she was trembling with a great sort of excitement. She looked up at him, and her eyes were swimming with moisture. "I knew it!" she said, almost to herself. "I knew I couldn't lose!"

She gave him a happy smile, pushed through the crowd, and went out into the street, followed by the envious glances of the less fortunate machine players. Ed was intrigued by the whole thing. The girl was so very evidently laboring under a terrific strain of some kind; it was quite chilly tonight, yet she wore nothing but a bathing costume that afforded her practically no protection.

He followed her out of the store. She was walking rapidly down Washington. Ed smelled activity, and he felt strangely elated. Here was mystery of some sort. And where there was mystery, you couldn't keep Ed away. He juggled revolvers on the stage for a living—a very good living. He was headlined from coast to coast as the Masked Marksman: "The Man Who Can Make Guns Talk." On the stage he performed feats of acrobatics and marksmanship that left the audience breathless at his sheer skill, the absolute mastery of the six forty-five caliber hair-trigger revolvers which were the props of his act.

Off the stage, he always carried two of those revolvers in the twin holsters under his arms. And his constant seeking after mystery and danger had often placed him in spots where he had all the need of the magic skill with firearms which he had developed in his years on the stage. For Ed needed excitement and danger the way the average man needs sleep. He dabbled in criminology the way other men might collect postage stamps and first editions. He had licenses in a dozen states to operate as a private detective, and his true name was known and feared in the underworld as much as his stage name was known and admired by the theatergoing public all over the country....

HE COULD see the girl now, heading south on Washington. His Drive-It-Yourself car, which he was going to turn in before taking the train, was parked at the curb. He hesitated a moment, debating whether to use the car or follow her on foot, and in that second of hesitation he felt his elbow gripped tight, turned to see a sallow faced, narrow eyed man in a palm beach suit. The man wore a pearl-gray fedora, had an expensive diamond in the white tie which rested on his black silk shirt. He was narrow shouldered and narrow waisted, and his lips were thin, stretched in a tight smile.

"I'd leave that girl alone, mister, if I were you!"

Ed started to twist his elbow out of the man's grip, but he suddenly felt something poked into his ribs on the other side. He stiffened, turned his head. Another man stood at his left, close to him. This man wore gray pants and a blue jacket. He had no hat, and black hair was combed sleekly back from a low forehead. His face was square, hard featured, and he held his left arm crossed over his stomach so that his left fist, with what he held in it, was jabbing Ed's side. Ed looked down, and saw the shimmering barrel of a gunmetal automatic in that fist. He raised his eyebrows.

The man with the automatic said: "That's good advice—what my friend gave you. You goin' to take it? Or do we take you?"

"Take me where?" Ed asked innocently.

"For a ride, guy, for a ride! Are you a sap? Don't you recognize the real business when you see it?"

Ed said dryly: "Yeah. I recognize the real business. What's the idea?" As he spoke he glanced furtively down Washington, made out the figure of the girl, more than a block away.

The man with the gun said tightly: "The idea is, we're kind of in a hurry, so you get a break. Scram, don't bother with that dame any more, and forget about this. Your health will be a whole lot better that way. Talk quick—yes, or no?"

Ed looked down at the gun, sighed: "Your argument is very forceful. I guess it ought to convince me."

The sallow man on the other side chuckled. "Smart man. Now you start taking a walk. Goodbye—and try to have a short memory."

Ed said: "Goodbye," and started to walk in the opposite direction from that taken by the girl, but toward his car. He heard the sallow man say to his companion: "Come on, Gilly. There won't be no trouble with him. He just got talking to her by accident—like I thought."

Ed walked down a little further, turned the corner, and then ducked into an alley that led him back to a second alley just behind the drug store. He poked his head out; saw the two men hurrying down Washington. He sprinted out, got into his car, backed, it away from the curb, made a complete turn in Washington in defiance of the traffic regulations of the City of Miami Beach, and raced the car after them. He passed the two men, but they didn't know it. They were walking very fast, their hands in their pockets, and their faces grim. Two blocks further down Ed spied the girl. She was just turning left off Washington, and he came up to the corner, made the left turn, too, crept along after her.

Looking back in the rear view mirror, he saw Gilly and the sallow man also turning the corner. The girl turned right on Ocean Drive, and then stopped before a doorway with a staircase leading upstairs from the street level. The sign outside the building which she entered read: PARKER'S BEACH CASINO.

Ed knew Parker's. It was a recently opened gambling room, set up in haste to catch some of the easy money from the spendthrift throngs that had flocked south this year. Parker controlled all the gambling and slot machine activities in Southern Florida. In this place he had installed roulette wheels, a blackjack layout and three dice tables. He also made book on the horse and dog races, and the jai alai games. There were no costly or elaborate decorations here, for the casino was in the cheaper section of Miami Beach, right around the corner from the Burlesque Theatre Pier. Along the street here, there were frankfurter stands, penny gambling stores, a second-rate boxing casino, and a couple of third-rate restaurants. The section was reminiscent of Coney Island's Bowery at its poorest. And it was here that this half-clad girl with the frightened eyes had come!

Ed swung his car into the parking lot across the street, threw his quarter to the attendant, and raced up the stairs of Parker's after her. Just before he entered, he cast a glance down the street, saw the sallow faced man and the man named Gilly turning the corner from First Street, and looking about them uncertainly. There were a dozen places the girl could have gone into, and they would have to stop into each of them before they got to Parker's.

Ed took the wooden steps two at a time, entered the big gaming room. The bare walls looked unwashed; the odor of cheap hamburger and onions came up from the restaurant below, pervading the place. But the eager faced, hot eyed men and women who thronged about the roulette and dice tables paid no attention to the walls, to the odors, or even to the occasional cockroaches that scampered across the bare floor. They were those who did not have the means or the appropriate clothes to attend the swankier gambling establishments on the Beach, and Parker had shrewdly opened this place to take care of them.

Ed cast his glance over the room, failed to spy the girl at first. She was not at the roulette table, neither was she at the thinly patronized blackjack table. The greatest crowd was at the dice tables, of which there were three. Ed pushed around, failed to find her at the first, which was the quarter minimum table, but found her at the second, where a dollar was the lowest permissible bet. She was standing close to the tall ladder on which sat the strong-arm man with the gun holstered at his side. She was breathing hard, and watching the man who was throwing the dice at the moment. Ed saw that she still clutched her quarters close to her breast.

THE DICE rolled on the table, and the house-man, standing on the other side of the table from the ladder, intoned: "Six! The gen'leman rolled a six, but eight's his point!" He deftly skimmed the dice back to the "gen'leman," using the long, curved rake, and skillfully avoiding the chips that were lying on the board. The "gen'leman" put the dice in the cup once more, rolled them out, and the houseman called out: "Seven! Seven to lose!" and raked in all the chips. "Who shoots next?" He looked around the table, and Ed saw the girl push forward, saying timidly: "Please, could I—roll them?"

The houseman grinned at her, while his eyes traveled over her abbreviated costume, as did the eyes of all the other men grouped around the table. There were some women there, and the women's glances were plainly contemptuous, sneering. The house-man said to her: "Sure, miss. You can have 'em!" He pushed the leather cup and the dice over to her, and she took her stack of quarters, laid them down in the box on the board marked: Win.

Ed was standing close behind her now, and he could almost feel her body tremble as she dropped the dice in the cup, started to shake them. The houseman pushed her quarters over to the cashier at the far end of the board, who counted them, substituted chips for them. Then the houseman pushed the chips back on the "Win" square. The girl took a deep breath, rolled the dice out of the cup with a half convulsive gesture. They bounced at the side boards, came to rest—with a five and a six showing!

The house-man announced: "Eleven! The lady throws a natural to win!" He deftly matched her stack of chips with another from his pile, pushed the two stacks over toward her, and raked the dice back. The girl shoved them all back on the square, picked up the dice again. She was letting them ride. Ed Race grinned sheepishly to himself, took out a ten dollar bill and put it on the "Win" square. He was going to ride with her. He sensed that some powerful need was driving her to do this, and he also sensed that there was a lucky streak running along with her tonight.

While the girl shook the dice, Ed kept his eyes on the entrance. The girl didn't know that he was behind her. If she knew that she had been followed by Gilly and the sallow faced man, she didn't show it. She never once glanced toward the door. She rolled out the dice, and there were amazed exclamations around the table. She had made another natural! The houseman called out: "Another eleven! The lady wins again!"

She had twenty dollars there, and she let it remain. Ed did the same with his twenty. Once more she rolled the dice. A six and a four—ten. Ed saw her face. She was pale, taut, as she cupped the dice to roll again. Ten was one of the two hardest points to make. Yet Ed felt sure she would hit it. He pulled out his roll of bills, placed a twenty in the next box. He would get odds of two to one if she made it. She rolled them out, and there it was—two fives! She had come right back with it.

The houseman said: "Ten and you win! Ten is the number. The lady made it the hard way!"

The girl now had forty dollars in chips. Ed had eighty, because he collected on his two-to-one bet in addition to the twenty he had bet to win. Ed watched her push all her chips into the box, and he did the same. Once more she rolled. Everybody around the table was watching her, but few were betting on her. The odds against her hitting three times in a row were too great. But she did. She hit another natural!

SHE LET her chips ride, and so did Ed. She saw Ed reaching out to shove his $160 worth of chips into the square, and she looked up at him, recognized him at once, and uttered a little gasp. Ed grinned down at her, said, "Go to it, sister. I'm right with you!"

She murmured: "You—followed me?" He evaded the question. "I drove over from the drug store, and I saw you here. I knew you were lucky tonight, so I figured I'd ride along with you."

She accepted his explanation, picked up the cup, and threw out the dice. Ed didn't watch them to see what they would show, for he had just caught a glimpse of Gilly and the sallow faced man, coming up the stairs. They stopped at the entrance, looked all around the place. Ed bent his head, so they wouldn't see him. And he heard the houseman announcing in awed tone: "The lady did it again! Another natural! Seven to win!" He pushed the huge stack of chips over toward her, and then pushed over Ed's stack. But when he raked the dice in her direction, she shook her head.

"I—I would like to pass the dice," she said. "I—want to cash in."

The house-man shrugged. "Okay, lady. But with your luck, you ought to push 'em.

The girl didn't answer, but went around to the end of the table while the houseman raked her chips over to the cashier. Ed motioned to him that he wanted to do the same, and followed her around. The cashier gave them each a slip—the girl's for $160 and Ed for $320. "Take 'em over to the office," he said, "and they'll give you the cash."

The girl said to Ed; "I'm glad you made money with me. It

was your nickels that started me off. I—need this money for—something special."

She started in the direction of the office, and stopped suddenly, her breath coming in quick, short gasps. Facing her were Gilly, and the sallow faced man, both with their hands in their pockets. The sallow faced man glanced up at Ed, said out of the side of his mouth: "Take care of the big palooka, Gilly," and reached out, gripped the girl's arm. "What you got there, Mrs. Frazer?" he asked, looking down at the pink slip in her hand.

The girl stood there, white-faced. She seemed paralyzed, unable to speak. Gilly came around on the other side of the girl, stood up close to Ed, with his right fist in his coat pocket, poking out at Ed. "You lookin' for trouble, huh?" he demanded.

Ed said mildly: "No, not at all, Mr. Gilly. I take it as it comes!" His left hand closed on Gilly's right wrist—the one that was in the big man's coat pocket—while his right fist came up in a smashing blow to the side of Gilly's jaw. Gilly's gun exploded in his pocket, the slug burning a searing streak of fire along his own trousers leg, then crunching into the wooden floor. At the same time, Gilly buckled over, slumped to the floor, moaning.

The sallow-faced man swung the girl around, dragging at his pocket, and shouting: "Take him, boys!"

Mrs. Frazer screamed to Ed: "Look out! They'll kill you! This is Parker!"

ED'S HANDS moved with the lightning speed that always characterized his actions on the stage. With eye defying speed, his two heavy forty-fives appeared. And almost with the same motion the gun in his left hand swept up, and then down, smacking against the bone of Parker's wrist as it came out of his pocket with a pistol. Parker dropped the pistol, still shouting: "Take him, boys!" The pistol clattered on the floor, and Parker leaped for it. Ed kicked him hard in the ribs, and he fell away from the weapon, rolling on the floor in agony. At the same time, a gun exploded back near the dice table, and a slug whined past Ed's head.

Ed swung, snapped a shot back, toward the man on the ladder, who had fired. The man uttered a scream, and toppled from the ladder. There were two more men on ladders at the two other dice tables, and they were both shooting at Ed. But when he swung his big forty-fives at them, they leaped from their high, exposed perches, took cover behind the tables, and kept on shooting.

The big room was in pandemonium now. Deafening explosions of the heavy caliber weapons rolled against the eardrums. Frightened men and women patrons milled around the place. Ed was straddling the fallen Parker, and trading shots coolly with the two men from the ladders, and with a couple of the housemen who had also produced guns. He shouted at the girl, who was standing there, dazed: "Get out! Quick!"

She shook her head, bent and picked up Parker's pistol, and started to shoot at the men who were firing at Ed. Ed grinned through the smoke. "Good kid!" he exclaimed, but his voice was drowned by the roar of his own forty-fives. He moved over a little, so that his body screened the girl's as much as possible. He fired coolly, methodically, not wasting his shots. The firing had diminished now, for the panic-stricken crowd, of patrons were all over the place, getting in the line of fire. Ed threw a shot at a head that showed over the edge of one of the dice tables, saw it disappear, then turned and seized the girl by the arm, ran with her toward the door, leaving Parker on the floor. There were no more shots now, but women were screaming, and men were shouting wildly.

Ed reached the head of the staircase, pushed a group of people out of the way, and ran down, still holding on to the girl's arm. He bolstered his own guns, snapped to the girl: "Wipe that gun off, and drop it there!"

She obeyed, wiping it against her shorts, and letting it fall to the stairs. Then they were out in the street. A crowd had gathered in front of the door, and a police whistle was shrilling somewhere around the corner. Excited voices demanded of them: "What's the matter? What's happening up there?"

Ed said: "There's a shooting match. Some gangsters upstairs."

The police whistle sounded closer, accompanied by the whine of a siren. Ed pushed through the crowd with the girl, got to the other side of the street, and steered her into the parking lot where he had left his car.

The street in front of Parker's was suddenly flooded with police. The parking lot attendant had run across to see what all the shooting was about, and Ed drove out, with the girl crouching next to him, without being observed. He headed toward Fifth Street, then over on to the County Causeway leading off the Beach, across Biscayne Bay, toward Miami proper.

The girl sat silently beside him, clutching the pink slip of paper which she had failed to cash in Parker's. Ed glanced at her, gave her his own slip to hold. The girl said: "Y-you're doing an awful lot for me—without even knowing who I am. The police will be looking for us both now. S-some of those men back in Parker's were—hurt!"

ED LAUGHED shortly, guiding the car expertly along the edge of the causeway. "I know who you are—now," he said. "You're Mrs. Hiram Frazer—the wife of the district attorney of Palm Beach County."

She uttered a little, startled gasp. "You—know?"

He nodded. "I heard Parker call you by name. Then I connected you up. I saw you last year at the Miami Biltmore, but I didn't remember you till he called you Mrs. Frazer." Ed slowed the car up, pulled up at the side of the road. A little beyond them was the flat ground of one of the several flying fields located on the causeway. These fields were all operated by fliers who took the public up for sightseeing trips over Miami, charging from two to three dollars per trip.

Mrs. Frazer looked back of them, through the rear window, apprehensively. "W-why are you stopping here?" she asked nervously. "They may be coming after us—"

"I'll tell you, Mrs. Frazer," Ed said seriously. "I got in a shooting scrape back there; I shot at least two men. Tonight I've got to go in to police headquarters and give myself up. I may have a tough time proving that I shot in self-defense. I may even go to jail. If I don't go to jail, I can at least expect to be held here for trial or until the district attorney gets good and ready to drop the case. And here you are, without any clothes and without any money. You need help. You're in some kind of jam. All right, I'll be glad to help you out if I can—but you'll have to tell me what it's all about. Why did Parker and that other bird follow you around? Why did they try to stop me when I came after you out of the drug store? And why are you parading around Miami Beach at night in that costume?"

She looked up at him diffidently. "It—it's all so terrible." She shuddered. "I didn't know men could be so vile!"

"That's fine for a starter," Ed told her. "Now let's get down to cases. There isn't much time. We're liable to hear a siren behind us any minute now."

"All right. I'll try to tell it as clearly as I can. My husband, Hiram, has been fighting the gambling and slot machine interests in Palm Beach for years now. Parker is so entrenched though, that Hiram has never been able to do anything about it. Now that the slot machines have been declared legal, Parker has spread out more than ever; he's been taking in almost a million dollars a week net out of the machines, let alone his various gambling houses. His machines are spread all over Dade and Broward and Palm Beach Counties."

"So far, so good. You haven't told me any news yet."

"I'm coming to it. Yesterday, a piece of evidence came into Hiram's hands. He learned that Parker is wanted as a fugitive from justice in Oklahoma! Parker escaped from the detention pen in Oklahoma City, just as he was to be put on trial for a post office robbery. He killed a guard and got away, and was never heard from since—that's more than four years ago."

Ed's eyes narrowed. "You're sure of that?"

SHE NODDED. "Uh-huh. Hiram got Parker's fingerprints

on his application to operate slot machines in Dade County. Parker must have grown careless, or else he's sure of himself—he handled that application, and left his prints on it. Well, Hiram was getting ready to swear out a warrant for Parker, but there must have been a leak in the office. While Hiram was away, two men came to my house—we live in Palm Beach—and they said that if I went with them to Miami they would furnish me with additional evidence that would help Hiram to wipe out every bit of gambling from Palm Beach to Key West. They said that if Hiram could do that, he'd be the next logical candidate for governor. I tried to get Hiram on the 'phone, but they must have known I wouldn't be able to. They said there was no time to waste—"

"So you went with them!" Ed broke in.

"Yes. They had a car. They told me I would have to pay money for the information, and I dug up fourteen hundred dollars that we had in the safe. We stopped at the Golden Beach Hotel, down on the ocean front, and the men said that the person who would give us the information was one of Parker's disgruntled employees, and was waiting for us up in room eleven. We went up there, and there was nobody in the room."

She shuddered, covered her face with her hands, spoke through her fingers. "T-they t-took away all my clothes. T-they had a camera, and t-they were going to take a p-perfectly t-ter-rible p-picture of me, and s-show it to Hiram, and if he exposed Parker they were going to p-publish the p-picture. It—it would have ruined Hiram politically."

"Who were those men?" Ed growled.

"Parker, and that other one who followed me. I—didn't know at the time that he was Parker—and there he had been, promising to get evidence against himself!"

"I take it you got away from them?" While she talked he had been busy loading his two revolvers, and he holstered them again.

"Parker held me, while the other one got the camera ready. I bit Parker in the hand, and got away from him, and ran into the next room, and bolted the door. I—I had no clothes on, and they were beating against the door. I—couldn't dare to call for help. Imagine if I'd been found there—the wife of Hiram Frazer, naked in a hotel room! I found this bathing suit, and put it on, and climbed out the window. I slid down the drain pipe in back of the hotel, and ran away. I didn't know whom to call on here in Miami; I couldn't tell who was with Parker, and who was against him. And if I'd gone to the police, it would have got in the papers. They'd taken my money too, of course. The only thing I could think of was to p-play the machines. That was when I asked you to let me try."

Ed chuckled. "Damned smart—making Parker's own machines get you the money to go back to Palm Beach with!"

"B-but I haven't got the money. All I have is this slip. And I need some clothes. Now, if we're caught," she hesitated, "Hiram is a very proper person. He would never understand—"

"You could tell him you'd been kidnapped—"

"That's right. I never thought of that. But then—these clothes—?"

She stopped as the shriek of a police siren cut through the

night from behind them on the causeway. She clutched at Ed's sleeve. "They're after us! Hurry—"

Ed shook his head. "We couldn't get away. We're bottled." He pointed ahead. The drawbridge on the causeway was slowly rising. "They must have 'phoned the bridge tender. And it wouldn't do us any good to get across. They've probably radioed ahead to the Miami police. There'd be a reception for us on the other side. We'll have to face it sooner or later. It might as well be now. You get down low. Don't show yourself for a while." She looked at him, puzzled, but obeyed.

TRAFFIC BEHIND them had opened up for the police patrol car. There were two patrolmen in it, and two men in plain clothes on the running boards. The police car was moving along slowly, the officers peering in at the occupants of the halted autos along the road. When they came abreast of Ed's car, one of the civilians shouted: "There he is?"

Ed saw that the two civilians were Parker and Gilly. Both had guns in their hands. Gilly was on the right-hand running board and Parker on the left.

The car braked to a halt, and the two officers, with Gilly and Parker, surrounded Ed's car. One of the officers thrust a gun out. "Put your hands up! Come outta there!"

Ed said: "Okay, officer. We were waiting for you. You know I shot in self-defense, don't you?"

"Yeh, we know that. That's what we was told by the crowd. But you ran away. You'll have to come back—"

Ed said steadily: "Okay. But take Parker back with you. He's a fugitive from justice from the state of Oklahoma."

The officer exclaimed: "Huh? How come?"

Parker started to laugh. "That's a swell story. He's trying to pull a fast one. I'm goin' on to Miami. I'll be back in the morning to press the charge against this guy—"

"You'll come back with us," Ed told him. "You're going to be held for extradition. Your game is up in Miami—and everywhere else, for that matter."

The cop nodded. "You might as well come back, Parker. You're a material witness. You claim he started the shooting. An' maybe there is something to this man's story about you being a fugitive from justice—"

Parker said softly to Gilly: "I guess we give it to them, Gilly. There's a flying field right over there. We can make a clean getaway. Let's go!"

Parker's and Gilly's guns spoke at the same instant. They each fired into the back of one of the officers. The patrolmen died on their feet, buckled to the ground with their guns unfired. But the shooting didn't end. Ed had moved with lightning speed, almost before Parker had stopped talking. His two forty-fives were out, in his hands, and blazing even as Parker and Gilly turned their own guns on him.

The deep throated roar of Ed's heavy revolvers drowned the spiteful cracks of the two criminals' pistols. Lead slammed into them with unerring accuracy, and they were hurled back, their fingers contracting wildly on their triggers, their shots going up in the air. Huge blobs of crimson appeared on their chests. Gilly was whirled around by the force of the shots that struck him, and fell on his face, twitched, then became motionless. Parker, with a slug in his chest and one in his heart, tottered for an instant, while the gun fell from his nerveless fingers; then he slowly bent at the waist. His knees buckled, and his mouth was set in a furious, dead snarl. In death, his face had assumed a venom which would remain as a mask of death. He collapsed, and the causeway became stained with red around his body.

Ed pushed out of the car, went around on the other side and opened the door for the girl, drew her Out. "Get over to the flying field!" he ordered. "There won't be anyone around this late. Go in the office and wait there for me. When I'm finished with the cops, I'll come back for you!"

As in a daze, she obeyed. It was several minutes before the scared motorists in the halted cars mustered up enough courage to approach. By that time, another police patrol car had arrived from the Beach, with Captain Stanley of the Beach Police Force. Stanley knew Ed, but even at that, Ed had to go back with him and with the bodies of the two cops and the two dead gunmen. It was another hour before they were able to match Parker's fingerprints and identify him as a fugitive from justice. It was one o'clock in the morning before the local district attorney, after a lot of wire pulling, agreed to release Ed in his own custody for the coroner's hearing in the morning.

CAPTAIN STANLEY accompanied Ed out of the station house. "You lucky stiff!" he grumbled. "You just happen in and grab yourself a guy that's wanted all over the country and that we had right here in our midst all this time! And the reward, too!" He sighed. "You don't need that dough either."

"I don't," Ed agreed. "And when I get it, I'm donating it to the Miami Beach Police Fund. Now I got to scram, if you don't mind—"

"Hey, wait a minute!" Stanley caught him by the sleeve. "There's something the D.A. forgot to ask you. Who was that dame, in the B.V.D.s, that was at Parker's? Was she with you? They said she picked up a gun—"

Ed shrugged. "Just a public-spirited bathing beauty. I hope I meet her again."

"You don't know who she is?"

Ed took Stanley's lapel in his fingers, said confidentially: "Listen, cap, I know her so well, I'm going up for an airplane ride with her right now. We're taking a little spin up to Palm Beach!"

Stanley grinned at Ed's departing back. "Always the kidder, ain't you, Race!"

DEATH STEALS THE ACT

ED RACE was making a speech of appreciation during a dinner at which he had just been announced the winner of a new motor car, when Death whispered in his ear. But Ed Race didn't know the dread significance of those words at first, nor did he recognize the deferential, dark clad headwaiter as a grim messenger of doom.

He paused frowning at the interruption. The headwaiter at his elbow thrust into his hand a portable telephone which had been plugged into the outlet in the dining room. "Call for you, Mr. Race."

"Don't you see I'm in the middle—"

The waiter was apologetic. "That's what I told the gentleman, sir. He's outside in the lobby of the hotel and insists on talking to you. I asked him to wait ten minutes, but he refused. He said that he might be dead in ten minutes."

Ed Race echoed: "Dead—in ten minutes?" He turned to the men around the table: "Excuse me, boys. This seems to be serious." He took the instrument from the waiter. "Hello! This is Race. Well?"

The voice of the man in the lobby was frantic.

"Mr. Race, I've got to see you at once. Can you come out here in the lobby—right away?"

"Listen," Ed growled. "I can't leave now."

"Please! My life is in danger!"

"And who are you?"

"You don't know me, but you must have heard of me. I'm John Delaney."

Ed whistled. "You mean, Mr. Partages' partner?"

"Yes, yes. He and I control the stock of the Partages vaudeville circuit. I just called Leon…. He told me I'd find you here…. I came over instead of phoning. I dare not go home. They may be watching—"

"Wait a minute," Ed interrupted. "I'll come out."

He handed the 'phone back to the waiter, said to the table of interested faces: "I'm sorry, boys, but this thing seems to be really important. I may not be able to come back—"

When Ed left the room, Silas Dean went out in the corridor with him while he got his hat and coat from the check girl. Ed put the coat on, felt of the two heavy forty-fives in the two inside pockets. He always carried those two guns. They were two of the six with which he performed so miraculously on the stage, and he never went without them. He carried them in his topcoat now—you can't wear forty-fives with evening clothes.

Dean called out to him as he left: "Don't forget to take your new car away, Race—you lucky stiff."

Ed grinned, waved to him, and walked out into the main lobby. He looked around at the men and women there, but saw no one who seemed to be awaiting him. He frowned, started over to the desk, then he heard a page boy calling: "Mr. Race, please. Mr. Race, please!"

He motioned the boy over, gave him a quarter, and took the note on the tray. He asked: "Who left this?"

"A skinny little gentleman, sir. He was in a hurry.... He went out with two other men."

Ed nodded, unfolded the note. It was scrawled, apparently in great haste:

"Dear Mr. Race:

I was unduly alarmed. I find I am really in no danger. Sorry I called you away from the dinner. I hope you'll overlook it.

John Delaney."

Ed grabbed the arm of the page boy, who was already moving off.

"Which way did those three men go, sonny?"

The boy pointed. "Out that way, sir. Not two minutes before you called me."

Ed hurried out the exit indicated. There were a good many people in the lobby, and he was a bit delayed in getting out. On the street, he glanced quickly up and down; saw the ornately dressed Astor doorman hurrying across the street toward the hotel, clutching two fat cigars in his hand. The doorman was looking in the direction of two men who were walking quickly east on Forty-Fifth toward Broadway.

ED HEARD the doorman shout: "Hey, mister, here I am. Here's the cigars you sent me for."

The two men near the corner turned, glanced behind them, one of them taking the cigars from the doorman. Then they started toward Broadway again. Ed Race's jaw tightened. He

had recognized one of the two men as they passed under a street light. He was Vic Krohn, once a bodyguard for the notorious alky baron, Mike Serrone, who was finishing up a long term at Alcatraz.

Ed started to run after them. Krohn, whether from instinct or caution, turned his head, saw Ed, said something to his companion, and then both men sprinted around the corner. Ed's long legs were carrying him swiftly after them. It was past nine o'clock, and Forty-Fifth Street was no longer congested by the theatre crowd. He would have made it, if it hadn't been for the doorman. The bulky fellow was standing on the side-walk, gazing at the fast retreating Krohn and companion when

Ed came tearing past. And it was just at that moment that the flunky began to move his lumber some form. He stepped to one side, collided with Ed, and the two of them went sprawling in the street. Ed cursed, sprang to his feet, and raced around the corner. He was too late. There was no sign of the two men in the moving Broadway crowd. They might have slipped into the moving picture theatre just off the corner; they might have gone down into the automat cafeteria. In either case they could easily slip out of a side entrance. Or they might even be among the congested throng on the street. It was impossible to spot them. And then, too, Ed had just acted on a hunch. He had nothing that he could really say or do to Krohn or the other man if he did catch them.

Disgustedly he turned back into Forty-Fifth to find the doorman picking himself up cumbrously. Ed said to him savagely: "Never mind introductions. Just tell me what those two men were doing!"

The doorman spattered: "W-why, nothing, sir. They came out of the hotel with another man. One of them gave me a dollar, and told me to go over to the cigar store, get him two El Perfectos and keep the change. I did…. You saw me give them the cigars. Then you slammed into me."

"Where'd the third man go?"

"I'm sure I don't know, sir. Now that you mention it, it is funny. There was only two of them just now."

"What did this third man look like?"

"I really couldn't tell you, sir. I didn't pay any attention to him."

Ed sighed. "All right. Here's a dollar. If that third man comes back, tell him I'll be waiting for him in the lobby." He left the puzzled doorman, entered the hotel again, and went into a 'phone booth. He called the home of Leon Partages, his boss, but the maid who answered the 'phone told him mat Mr. Partages was not at home.

"He's gone to an important director's meeting, Mr. Race," she informed him. "It's at Mr. John Delaney's home, in the Princess Apartments, on Riverside Drive. Mr. Partages was trying to get you on the 'phone at the Astor a few minutes ago, but they told him you'd already gone. He left word to tell you to call him at Mr. Delaney's home. The number is Torquemada 7-1224."

Ed thanked her, hung up, and dialed Delaney's number. He knew that Partages lived only around the corner from the Princess Apartments and should be there already. In fact, Partages was just entering Delaney's apartment when Ed asked for him. The boss of the vaudeville circuit took the 'phone.

"Listen, Mr. Partages," Ed stormed, "what kind of a nut did you wish on me? This Delaney—"

"Yes, yes, Eddie," Partages broke in excitedly. "What about him? Is he safe? Did you talk to him?"

"No. He 'phoned from the lobby here that he wanted to talk to me, but when I got out he was gone. He left me a note saying that he couldn't stay—that it was all wrong about his being in danger. I understand he left with two other men. Maybe he was snatched!"

Partages groaned. "It's terrible, Eddie. You've got to find him for me. Get hold of Delaney inside of half an hour and bring him here! My God, I've got to have him!"

"What's it all about, Mr. Partages?"

"My God, they're going to take the whole circuit away from me! I built it up from one nickelodeon theatre twenty-five years ago till now we've got four hundred houses all over the country.... And they're going to take it away from me!"

"How?"

"How? By voting me out. I own forty percent of the stock and Delaney owns fifteen percent. Some racketeers got their hands on the rest. That's what this special stockholders' meeting is for. They're going to elect another chairman in my place and throw me out on my ear!"

ED SCOFFED. "Don't tell me that racketeers could get together enough money to buy up three million dollars' worth of stock—"

"No, no, Eddie, they didn't buy it. They got proxies. They scared the small stockholders into giving them proxies. Delaney and I together control enough votes to save the business. You got to get Delaney!"

"I'll do my best," Ed said dubiously.

"No, Eddie, you got to do better than that. I never asked you for such a favor before—but I'm asking one now because I might lose everything.... Eddie, you've *got* to get me Delaney. That damn lawyer for the racketeers is here now, and he's gloating all over. He knows that something has happened to Delaney."

"Who is it?" Ed demanded.

"It's Pringle—Lee Pringle!"

"Hell!" Ed exclaimed. "Pringle is a criminal lawyer. He used to be the mouthpiece for Mike Serrone before the Big Shot was sent to Alcatraz. Is *he* in this deal?"

"Yes! Sure! I told you it was a bunch of racketeers. They're going in for high finance racketeering, now that their old games are busted up. They'll milk the company dry in six months and then let it go. Ed, you've got to help me save the business I've spent a lifetime building up!"

"Listen, Mr. Partages," Ed rapped into the 'phone. "You hang on there. Try to stall them off from voting. I'm coming right up. In the meanwhile call the police and send out an alarm for Delaney."

"But what can you do up here, Eddie?"

Ed Race's lips were tight, his eyes bleak. "Maybe I can show Pringle that it would be healthier for him to postpone the Board meeting!"

Ed hung up, stalked out of the booth into the lobby. He was sweating. The close quarters of the booth had been hot. In addition, the night was warm and he was wearing a topcoat, the pockets weighed down by two forty-fives.

He pushed through the lobby, came out on Forty-Fifth, and said to the doorman: "Get me a cab—quick! No! Hey, wait!" He snapped his fingers. "I clean forgot! I own a car now. There's supposed to be a new Gibraltar sedan parked down here!"

"It's right over there, sir, down by the employees' entrance. Did you win it, sir? Mighty lucky... say, that's funny! There's someone driving it away!"

Ed saw the new, shiny, maroon colored Gibraltar being eased away from the curb.

There was a man at the wheel, another beside him. Ed glimpsed the rear license plate; saw that it was a dealer's number beginning with DL. He shouted "Hey, you!" and started running after the car, which had already accelerated its way west toward Eighth Avenue.

The driver and his companion did not look around. Ed kept running, the doorman beside him. The doorman exclaimed breathlessly: "These auto thieves only pick the best, sir. A brand new car like that."

Ed wasn't listening. He made his way out into the middle of the street and pulled his right hand revolver. The man beside the driver in the Gibraltar looked behind, saw Ed, and whispered to the driver who hunched over the wheel. The car spurted forward. There was a red traffic light at the corner of Eighth Avenue and half a dozen cars were waiting for it to change, blocking off the Gibraltar. The car thieves could not hope to get away.

Suddenly the sedan came to a sharp stop. The two men flung the doors open, one on each side, and leaped out into the street, fled, one to the right and the other to the left. Startled passersby paused to stare at the running men, and at Ed Race bearing down on them. One of the two men reached the sidewalk, turned, a gun in his hand. He raised it to fire at Ed, snapped a shot which went high and wide, and then turned toward the entrance of a nearby hotel. Ed threw a quick shot at him and caught the man in the fleshy part of the right leg.

The man keeled over, sprawled on the pavement, just as a patrolman came puffing up. The second thief had disappeared. A crowd gathered about the fallen man, Ed having to push his way through. The wounded man was gasping. Though the wound was only a superficial one, the breath had been knocked out of him. A slug from a forty-five does that. He was bleeding profusely.

The patrolman was tugging at his own gun, having difficulty in getting it out as he eyed Ed apprehensively. He no doubt thought that Ed was a gunman, and that he was witnessing a gang fight.

Ed reassured him. "It's all right, officer. You don't have to worry. This man was stealing my car over there."

The patrolman rapped: "Well, we'll see. Give us that revolver of yours till I check up on the story."

Ed shrugged, handed him the gun. The wounded man on the sidewalk snarled "He's lying, officer. I never touched his car. He tried to hold me up—and when I tried to defend myself, he shot me."

Ed broke in: "Save it, pal. You're wasting your breath. The doorman of the Astor saw you driving off with the car. Here he is."

THE POLICEMAN was still scratching his head in perplexity when the house physician of the hotel came rushing out. He knelt beside the wounded man. "It's nothing serious," he said. "If you can get him upstairs to my office, you won't even have to call an ambulance. I can fix him up."

Several men from the crowd volunteered to carry the man up. Ed bent to help but the cop gripped his arm, pulled him back. "No you don't, guy. You wait right here till the sergeant comes along."

Traffic had started to move and was sending up a furious

honking of horns. The Gibraltar was still out in the middle of the street. Ed said: "Let me move the car out of the way."

"Nix. You just stand still!"

Just then a squad car pulled in to the curb and Sergeant Dave Sayre got out. Ed breathed a sigh of relief. He knew Sayre well. He buttonholed the sergeant. "Look, Dave," he said hurriedly, after detailing the events of a few moments before. "I'm in one hell of a hurry. I've got to get uptown, pronto. Here's the Astor doorman who will corroborate everything I've told you. Hold that wounded bird till I finish my business uptown, then I'll come down and sign any papers you want…. But for the love of Pete, don't hold me up any longer. It's damned important!"

Sayre nodded. "Go ahead, Race." He motioned to the cop. "Give Mr. Race his gun…. And get upstairs to the doctor's office. Put that wounded guy under arrest and hold him there. What's the idea of lettin' him go up without a guard?"

The cop's face got red. "Gee, sergeant, I didn't know which one to hold onto. This was the guy that done the shootin', so I figured he was—"

"All right, all right! Get up there before that egg gets bandaged up and scrams!"

The cop left. Ed thanked Sergeant Sayre, promised to stop in at the precinct house before midnight, and went over to the sedan. He didn't have to use the key that Silas Dean had given him because the motor was still running. As he got behind the wheel, Sayre, who had walked over with him, asked: "What about this guy, Delaney? You think Krohn was in on the snatch? Should we pick him up?"

"Not yet, Dave. Tell you what—after you're through here, you come up to Delaney's place at the Princess Apartments on Riverside Drive. We can start from there. Thanks for cutting the red tape…. Hm-m-m—now let's see how this new bus goes."

Sayre looked the car over. "How come, Race? You always said you preferred to use cabs. Why the investment?"

Ed grinned. "It was wished on me, Dave. I won it in a raffle. And before I get to drive it, it's stolen on me I…. So long!"

He shifted into first, drove off, and headed uptown on Eighth Avenue. The car was a honey. It ran smoothly, accelerated beautifully. The motor purred like a thoroughbred. The thief had evidently spliced two of the ignition wires to start her up, for the ignition switch was still locked. Ed stepped on the gas all the way up to Seventy-Second. He frowned as his ears caught a faint throb that seemed to come from the rear end. He shrugged. The car had cost him only two dollars. He could afford to spend a few dollars to fix her up. But anyway, she should carry a new car guarantee, even though he hadn't paid for her.

Ed swung west at Seventy-Second. Taking the curve, the throb in the rear was even more pronounced, but, somehow, he paid no attention to it. He was thinking of the situation in which Leon Partages found himself. Pringle would be a tough customer to handle. He drove two blocks up Riverside Drive and pulled in at the curb in front of the Princess Apartments. He said to the doorman who held the door open for him: "I've got to leave the motor running. See that no one takes her, will you?"

He slipped the doorman a dollar, hastened inside and entered the elevator. "Mr. Delaney's apartment," he said.

The operator grinned. "Mr. Delaney is on the ground floor, sir. Apartment two."

Ed left the elevator, crossed the lobby and rang the bell of apartment two. The door was opened by Vic Krohn.

Krohn was smiling thinly. He had a small automatic at his hip, and was holding it so that the muzzle winked up at Ed. He said: "Come in, sucker. You're expected."

Ed stood loosely, his hands at his sides, touching the two heavy forty-fives through the cloth of his coat pockets. He said mildly: "That was a quick getaway you made over at the Astor. What'd you do with Delaney?"

KROHN'S SMILE vanished. He glowered. "I don't know what you're talking about. Come inside and quit the gabbing."

Ed nodded and walked in past Krohn who backed into the foyer. Krohn reached around, slammed the hall door shut and motioned with the automatic. "Go right inside, Race. The meeting will start in five minutes."

Ed turned slowly, entered the large sitting room. Four men were seated there. A library table near the wall had been cleared of books and a lamp which were piled on the floor. At the table sat the thin faced, sharp-nosed lawyer, Lee Pringle, whom Ed knew and disliked thoroughly. Leon Partages was sitting stiffly in a straight-backed chair, sweating a little. His ordinarily good-natured face bore a gloomy aspect and his pudgy hands were twining and untwining in his lap. Near the window sat the man whom Ed had seen with Krohn at the Astor. He was a thickset, heavy-jowled fellow. He was chewing tobacco, spitting on the rug. He had a finger through the trigger guard of a gun, swinging it.

It was the fourth man in that room that interested Ed. The fourth man was sitting at Pringle's right, smoking a cigar. He was thin, with a high forehead; coal black hair and coal black eyes. His hair was combed straight back from his forehead. He was attired in a natty light blue suit with a faint pinstripe and a blue shirt with a striped tie to match. There was a large diamond stick pin in the tie. He had his legs crossed, revealing pearl-gray spats. This man nodded pleasantly to Ed, said coolly: "Sit down, Race. We heard Partages talking to you on the 'phone in the foyer. Now, just don't make any trouble for us, and you won't get hurt. See?"

Ed felt Krohn's presence right behind him. He disregarded the gunman, and let his unflinching gaze meet the sharp black eyes of the seated man. "Hello, Mike," he said flatly. "How long since you got out of Alcatraz?"

Partages, who had been sitting tautly, saying nothing as Ed entered under the gun of Krohn, now started violently in his seat. "Alcatraz!" he exclaimed.

Ed nodded. "Sure, Mr. Partages. "Didn't you know that this gentleman is Mike Serrone, former Public Enemy Number One? He was up for a seven year stretch in Alcatraz on income-tax evasion charges. With time off he was due to come out about now, and the government wasn't announcing it to the press because they don't want to give these gangsters any more publicity than they can help."

Serrone stirred uncomfortably in his chair. Pringle, the lawyer, adjusted the glasses on his thin nose, coughed, and spoke. "Look here, Mr. Race, Mr. Serrone is my client. You be careful how you talk about him. You have called him a gangster. He could sue you for slander. He was convicted of evading income tax payments, and not of being a gangster. He is now engaged in legitimate business undertakings."

Ed's eyes were still locked with those of Serrone, but he said to Pringle: "Make the most of it, counselor. I still call your client a gangster. Why the guns? Does a legitimate business man carry two hoods like Krohn and this other guy?"

Pringle started to talk again, but Serrone silenced him with a raised hand. The gang leader got up daintily, rested one hand on the desk, where the big diamond ring on his little linger reflected the brilliance of the electric lights.

He said smoothly, "Enough of this. Race, you're too damn hot-headed. That's why I have Krohn and Milo here with their guns out you're liable to go off halfcocked. I want you to understand that we're here on legitimate business—we're attending a board of directors' meeting of the Partages Circuit. Krohn, Milo and I control forty-five percent of the voting stock. We've got all our proxies here, and we're ready for the meeting to begin. We're not starting any rough stuff unless you do—but we can hand it out if you want it that way. You may be handy with guns but Krohn and Milo can take care of you."

Ed laughed shortly. "How'd you get those proxies? You intimidated people into signing them. And now you want to take the business away from Mr. Partages. It's a new kind of racket!"

Serrone's eyes flickered. He glanced meaningly toward Krohn

who stood behind Ed, then at Milo who grinned and arose to stand with his gun pointing toward Ed. Then Serrano said coolly: "You're behind the eight ball, Race. We ain't violating any law here. It's you that's on the wrong end of it this time. Tell him, Pringle!"

THE LAWYER cleared his throat, fiddled with papers on the desk. "That is entirely so, Mr. Race. You must understand that this is an orderly Board meeting. It was called at the request of the proxy holders of forty percent of the stock, as provided in section eighteen of the bylaws of the corporation. There is nothing underhanded about this procedure. Why, even now, if Mr. Delaney should appear his shares, combined with those of Mr. Partages, could beat my clients. And furthermore, I tell you that Mr. Serrone, Mr. Krohn and Mr. Milo are all my clients, and I shall see to it that they obtain full satisfaction in the courts for the abuse you have heaped on their heads!"

Ed grinned. "That's a swell speech, Pringle. To listen to you anyone would swear that butter wouldn't melt in your mouth. But you know damn well that your clients are crooks and racketeers. You know damn well that Delaney's been either kidnapped or killed and that he won't show up here to cast his vote. You know that Krohn and Milo took him away from the lobby of the Astor while he was waiting for me."

Pringle shrugged. "Those are idle words. You could never prove anything in court. I think, Mr. Serrone, that if you have everything ready, we can go ahead with the business of the meeting. I shall act as secretary."

Ed looked across at Leon Partages, whose face was white.

Partages half rose from his chair. "You can't get away with this, Pringle!" he exclaimed. "We'll bring action in the supreme court to cancel this vote. We'll charge fraud, intimidation!"

Pringle smiled in superior fashion. "There is no fraud or intimidation, Mr. Partages. No one is compelling you to *vote* against your wishes. Your vote will be honestly recorded, I assure you."

Ed Race said flatly: "No it won't, Pringle. It won't be recorded at all." He twisted sideways with lightning swiftness. His elbow caught Krohn's wrist, slammed it to one side just as the automatic in Krohn's hand exploded. The slug thudded into the big desk. Milo fired, but Ed had gone into a back somersault just like the one he did on the stages of the Partages Circuit every day in the year. Milo's bullet went high over Ed's hurtling body.

Ed landed on his feet, lithely, over near the window. Two heavy forty-fives had appeared in his hands with magic speed. Ed Race, the Masked Marksman of the stage, was putting on a private exhibition of shooting which the theatre going public would have paid fifty dollars a ticket to witness. On the stage he juggled six heavy guns, did a back somersault, caught the guns as they came down into his hands and shot out the flames of a row of candles thirty feet across the stage. That was swift, accurate, precise marksmanship. This was easier for him, though it would have thrilled any audience—for his targets were live ones. Krohn and Milo died simultaneously, each with a slug in his forehead. Neither had a chance to shoot a second time.

Partages and Pringle sat rooted in their chairs. But Mike Serrone now showed the quick thinking energy that had brought him to the top of the heap in the rackets. He had a small pistol in his hand as he leaped behind Partages' chair. He seized the theatre proprietor by the back of his coat collar and pushed the muzzle of the pistol out over Partages' shoulder.

Ed was on the floor, past the startled face of Partages, looking almost directly into that small muzzle. Partages shrieked: "Shoot, Ed! Don't mind me!" And at the same time he jerked his right shoulder up just at the moment Serrone fired. Serrone's pistol was deflected, the slug whined at an angle, and lodged in the heart of the lawyer, Pringle. Pringle uttered a single short gasp, then a shriek, and fell over the desk. His shriek was drowned out by the deep throated roar of Ed Race's big forty-five. Ed's slug, fired from the floor, cleared Partages' shoulder by a split fraction of an inch and caught Serrone in the temple. It didn't leave a neat, round hole. It took off half the gang czar's head.

Partages got out of his chair, shaking as with the ague. Ed got to his feet, slipped the two guns back into his overcoat pocket. He surveyed the room full of dead men. "Hell!" he said. "That was a swell election."

Partages was clutching at his sleeve. "You shouldn't have done it, Ed! They had the law on their side. You'll be arrested. There's no crime we can pin on them. My God, why didn't you let them take the circuit away from me? I'd rather be a pauper than see you tried for murder, Eddie!"

Ed patted the stout man's shoulder. "And I'd rather do it this way, Mr. Partages. If we can prove they kidnapped or killed Delaney, I'll have a damn good defense!"

"But where in God's earth is Delaney?"

He stopped, and they both became conscious that the door bell was being rung steadily, loudly and raucously. The echoes of the thunderous shots had drowned out the door bell's sound and they didn't know how long it had been ringing. Now it stopped. A voice thundered: "Open up in there or we'll shoot the door in!"

Partages said breathlessly: "The police! What'll we tell them?"

Ed shrugged. "The truth. I think we're getting a break. That's Dave Sayre's voice if I'm not mistaken."

HE WENT out in the foyer, opened the hall door. Sergeant Sayre with a bluecoat behind him fairly hurled himself in, stopped short when he saw Ed Race. He had a gun but he lowered it. "Hell!" he exclaimed. "No more action?"

Ed grinned. "It's all over, Dave. I shot three men. But you'll find four stiffs in there."

Sayre grunted. "You're getting better and better. Now you shoot three, and kill four—*whew!*" He whistled softly as he stepped into the living room, past the white-faced Partages. His eyes swept the scene of carnage. "Mike Serrone, Krohn, Milo—and Pringle! My God! Race, what's been going on here? I hope you have the goods on these babies!"

"I haven't, Dave," Ed said quietly. "I only suspect that they've either kidnapped or killed John Delaney."

Sayre swung around and looked at Ed somberly. "You know what this means, Race? These birds—Pringle included—are no loss to society. But if you can't show evidence that they were engaged in the commission of a felony, you'll have to stand trial for shooting them. I'll have to take you in."

Partages broke in. "See here, sergeant, I witnessed the whole thing. It was self defense. I'll get the best lawyers in the country."

Sayre interrupted him. "Did they start the shooting?"

"Well, they had guns out…."

"Yeah. I know. And Race bucked the guns. It's a habit of his. Why did they have guns out?"

"Because they wanted to keep me from interfering in their damn board meeting," Ed told him. "I'm not going to try to lie out of this, Dave. I came up here, and you know it, to try to hold them off till maybe Delaney could show up."

Sayre said slowly: "Look, Race, I'm a hundred percent for you. You've done me plenty of favors. I'd advise you to change that story. The way it lines up now, you'll go to the chair. I've got to take you in, but you let Mr. Partages get you a couple of damn good lawyers and…."

He stopped as loud, excited voices came to them from the street, outside the window. The bluecoat, who had remained in the foyer, went to the front door. Ed jumped to the window, pulled back the curtain, looked out for a minute and then began to laugh.

Sayre frowned. He and Partages stepped up to the window and peered out too. Ed said to them: "There's my defense!"

He was pointing to the thin, bedraggled, bloody headed man being helped out of the back seat of the new Gibraltar sedan that Ed had left at the curb.

Partages shouted: "Delaney! Delaney!"

Ed opened the window and they all leaned out. The bluecoat

from the house came to the aid of the doorman, and together they supported the weak, shaky Delaney. He could hardly stand.

Delaney looked up at Ed, Sayre and Partages in the window and waved feebly. Partages called out to him: "What happened to you, John? How'd you get in that car?"

Delaney called to them in a voice that barely carried: "Those two men that took me from the Astor. They sent the doorman away, pushed me into the back of the car, and slugged me. I came to while the car was being driven…. I banged my heels against the floorboard but the driver didn't hear…. I was tied up, gagged, and couldn't get free. I just now smashed the glass. This man untied me."

Ed was grinning. "Can you beat it," he said. "And I thought there was a knock in the rear end!"

Sayre motioned to the bluecoat: "Bring Mr. Delaney up here. We want him to identify those two men who took him out of the Astor."

Delaney exclaimed: "You mean you got them upstairs? Man! Hold 'em. Don't you let them get away!"

"Don't worry," Sayre told him. "They won't get away. Mr. Race has seen to that!" The sergeant turned to Ed. "You always were a lucky stiff," he said. "You might have gone to the chair if Delaney hadn't turned up."

Ed gazed thoughtfully at the bodies of Krohn and Milo. "I really ought to thank those two for delivering my alibi all tied up like that. Come to think of it," he added, "it's a damn good thing I won that Gibraltar. If I hadn't come out looking for it when I did, those two lads would have carted it away. And then Delaney might never have been found!"

"Trust you," said Sayre, "to arrive at the right time. I bet when you finally do kick off the devil will run short of coal for his fires!"

DEATH GOES ON THE ROAD

IT WAS eight o'clock Sunday evening when Ed Race got off the train at Carrolltown. He went back to the baggage car, secured his two suitcases, had the porter carry them to a waiting taxi.

He said to the taxi driver: "Stop at the Partages Theatre so I can drop off one of these bags, then take me to the Carrolltown Hotel." He was about to get in when he felt a soft hand on his arm. He turned to find a young woman smiling at him. She was pretty in a plump sort of way, dark-haired, full-lipped. But there was a hard look in her eyes that Ed didn't particularly like.

She said: "You're Ed Race, aren't you?" Then, without waiting for his acknowledgment: "Suppose you let the cab wait. I'd like to talk to you."

There was a strange sort of assurance about her. And as if taking it for granted that he would acquiesce, she turned away. "There's a restaurant across the street. We can talk in there."

Ed's eyes narrowed. "Just a minute.... I don't know you. What do you want to see me about?"

It was a warm evening, and the girl was wearing a thin dress that set off her figure to advantage. It wasn't a bad figure, and she made the most of it. She came up close to Ed, so that he caught a faint scent of the perfume she used, and said softly: "I'm not trying to make you, Big Boy. This is business—the same busi-

124

ness that brings you here tonight. Let the taxi wait. You'll find it worth while."

Ed shrugged, said to the driver. "Okay, you wait for me." He then followed her across the street. Carrolltown was a fairly large place, being a county seat. It had grown up around the railroad station, the main street running off at an angle from the square in front of the depot. Two blocks away, Ed could see the huge sign of the Partages Theatre. Standing on a ladder was a man at work on the lettering of the marquee. Ed knew that man was probably putting up the streamer which would announce the appearance of the Masked Marksman—"The Man Who Can Make Guns Talk."

That was the way Ed Race was billed in every theatre of the Partages and allied circuits, from coast to coast. The marvelous skill and dexterity with guns which he demonstrated on the stage had won for him nation-wide popularity. His gun juggling and acrobatic act was headlined wherever it appeared—and the things he could do with those six heavy forty-five automatics of his never failed to bring down the house. Few knew his true identity off-stage, for he always appeared with a mask.

That this woman knew him was cause for concern. Only one person in Carrolltown was supposed to know that he was here for an additional purpose besides that of entertaining the public. And that one person was not this woman.

Moving casually across the street after her, Ed shrugged his broad shoulders forward just a little, thus easing his coat away from the twin holsters under his armpits where he carried two of the automatics which he used in his act. He noticed that a tall man who had been standing near the cab was also crossing the street, and that another man, with a slight limp due to a stiff leg, was moving down from the corner toward the restaurant. Both men had their hands in their jacket pockets, and were glancing furtively toward him.

The woman said nothing until they entered the "Golden Pheasant" and a waiter had shown them to a table. Ed saw that the two men were also coming in and taking a table toward the front. The woman had so maneuvered that Ed would sit opposite her, with his back to these two men. Ed made no objection and sat down facing her. She smiled at him, looked at a menu, and said to the waiter: "A ham sandwich on white bread and a cup of coffee."

Ed nodded. "Double it."

The waiter left and Ed rested his elbows on the table, studied the woman. Under the stronger light of the restaurant he saw that she was in her early thirties. Her face was full, on the verge of taking on more fat, but her skin was soft, her nose straight, and her mouth well-shaped. Her black hair was done in a bun in back, and she wore the blouse of her dress cut low in front to reveal a white, soft skin.

She let him study her for a moment, then said: "Well, Big Boy, how do you like me?"

Ed frowned. "You invited me in here to talk. All right, talk."

She made a face at him. "Always the business man, huh? Don't you ever play?"

He didn't smile. "I'm not playing now, thank you."

She flushed. "All right, all right. I'll get down to business.

And here's the business." She opened her purse and took out a thickly stuffed envelope, placed it on the table. Ed caught a glimpse of the butt of a small revolver in the purse. She saw his eye on it, and her lip curled. "You carry two guns, don't you?" she challenged.

Ed said: "You seem to know a lot about me. I don't even know your name. Suppose you talk."

"The name is Robinson, Big Boy. In case you want more, the first name is Elsie. *You* can call me Elsie any time you want."

"All right, Elsie. What's in the envelope?"

"Open it and see."

Ed smiled faintly, shook his head. "No. You open it."

"Cagey, huh?" She shrugged "Okay, Big Boy. I see they didn't overrate you when they said you were the works. Here goes...."

She used the knife the waiter had left, slit the envelope, and showed the contents to Ed without taking them out. The envelope was full of currency. She slipped the edge of one of the bills out—an engraved "100" showed in the corner.

"They're all the same, Big Boy—fifty of them. Five grand! Does it look good to you?"

"Is it all for me?"

Her eyes were bright. She pushed the envelope along the table. "Take it, Big Boy. Stow it away. It's all for you."

"Why?"

She looked disgusted. "Listen, don't act dumb. Do I have to spell it out for you?"

Ed smiled. "They say money talks—but in this case you better add a little explanation."

The waiter came with the coffee and sandwiches, and they were silent until he had gone. Then she said: "All right, if you got to have it that way. You're Ed Race, the Masked Marksman, and you work for Leon Partages. But you're more than an actor. You're so good with guns that Partages uses you every time there's a jam somewhere in his circuit. You were supposed to appear in Masonville next week, but Partages switched your booking so you could come to this town. Am I right?"

"Go on," Ed murmured. "You seem to be well informed."

Down at the far end of the restaurant there was a mirror on the swinging kitchen door. In that mirror Ed Race could watch the two men at the table behind him—and he saw that they were sitting tensely, keeping their eyes on himself and the woman. They still had their hands in their pockets.

Elsie Robinson went on: "The reason why Partages switched your booking, was because he just got an offer in New York of two hundred and fifty thousand dollars for the land and buildings of the Partages Theatre here in Carrolltown. The theater has been losing money for six months. He was tempted to sell—but he sent you here to look things over and find out if there was anything phony in the set-up. You're supposed to meet Harry Semple, the local manager of the Partages Theatre, in a room that's been reserved for you at the Carrolltown Hotel."

"Where do you fit into the picture?" Ed asked her. "And why this five grand?"

She tapped the envelope with a pink fingernail. "That's for you. Take it, and get on the long distance 'phone and tell Partages that it's okay for him to close the deal in New York. That's all you have to do for the five grand."

"You want me to do that before I even see Semple?"

"Yes…. And don't worry where I figure in the picture. I'm being paid to contact you."

"How did you find out all this about me? Everything you say is true. But no one is supposed to know why I'm here. Mr. Partages talked to me on the long distance at Masonville this morning, and I'm pretty sure nobody listened in."

She smiled. "You're asking too many questions, Big Boy. How about the deal?"

"Sorry, Elsie, it's no deal."

Her dark eyes narrowed, her lips pursed. "That final?"

"Uh-huh."

"And you're going to see Semple?"

"Right." Ed finished his coffee, raised a hand to the waiter for his check.

The woman stood up abruptly. She picked up the envelope and stuffed it in her purse. "So long, Big Boy," she said tauntingly. "Don't say I didn't try." And she walked swiftly away from the table.

As if it had been a signal, the two men behind Ed stood up, pushing back their chairs. The waiter was approaching from the rear of the restaurant, and the two men started moving toward Ed from the front. There were only one or two patrons in the restaurant at that late hour of the evening, and the two men attracted little attention. Their hands came out of their pockets very inconspicuously, but Ed, looking through the mirror on the kitchen door, saw that those hands held compact, flat automatics.

The waiter laid the check on the table and went away. Ed, keeping his eyes on the reflection of the two men, rose slowly, and crossed his arms over his chest, his capable fingers gripping the heavy stocks of the two forty-fives in his shoulder holsters.

The two men came up close on either side of him, and the one on the left, the one with the limp, said: "This is a gun I'm poking in your side, mister. My pal is got one on the other side. You can put down the money for the check an' walk out of here peaceable with us—or you can take it here. It's all one to us."

Ed's hands had slipped out of the holster, each gripping a gun, the long blued-steel barrels were by his elbows. His arms were still crossed, and he appeared to be standing very negligently. He glanced amusedly from one to the other of the two men, saw that their automatics were jammed up against his sides. He sighed, said: "You fellows certainly are careless." He stepped back slowly, and he saw that the man with the game leg was grinning, thinking that he had capitulated.

But, instead of turning around and walking out, Ed suddenly brought the barrels of his two guns down in a slapping motion, with unerring accuracy. They cracked against two wrists with a sickening, crunching sound, and two automatics fell to the floor. One exploded, the slug tearing into the leg of the table. The noise of the explosion sounded like thunder in the enclosed restaurant, and the diners at the two other occupied tables sprang up in panic, while the waiters huddled in a corner near the rear. The cashier screamed.

Ed kicked the two automatics across the floor, holstered his own guns, and grinned at the two gunmen, who were staring at him stupidly, holding onto their wrists. "Now," he said, "you boys will kindly sit down until the cops arrive. And then, maybe you'll do a little talking."

The sound of his voice was drowned by the sudden staccato chattering of a machine gun outside. Glass windows were shattered, and slugs screamed into the restaurant, smashed the mirror on the kitchen door, tore into the walls. The hail of lead was quickly sweeping toward the spot where Ed and the two men stood, moving like a flailing scythe of destruction. Ed acted with all the speed and coördination of muscle, mind and eye that characterized his movements on the stage, where he nightly snatched juggled guns out of the air and fired them at the flames of a row of candles forty feet across the stage. He had never missed a candle in eight years of vaudeville juggling marksmanship, and he didn't miss now as the two forty-fives leaped into his hands again with eye-defying speed and began to blast at the sedan at the curb, from which the barrage of machine gun lead was storming.

Six times in quick succession each of those heavy automatics roared out their deep-throated defiance of the chattering Tommy gun. Ed's slugs drew a straight line across the side of that sedan, parallel to the spot where the black snout of the machine gun poked out of the window. And the chattering stopped with decisive suddenness. The snout of the machine gun disappeared. Abruptly, quiet descended upon the restaurant and the street.

The quiet lasted only a moment. Screams began to keen out in the street, shrilling high above the muted groans of a man who lay upon the floor, writhing in an ever widening pool of blood. He was one of the innocent diners at a table near the window, and he had been caught in the first blast of the machine gun. Another diner was slumped over a table, the back of his head literally blasted off, his arms stretched across the cloth, the water from an overturned glass adulterating the deep crimson which was saturating the tablecloth. The restaurant was a shambles of blood and wrecked furniture. Waiters came out timidly, and two of them went into the street to look at the sedan which had not moved from its spot at the curb.

Ed loaded his automatics with swift, dexterous fingers, and

glanced about for the two men who had tried to hold him up. They were gone.

The cashier, a peroxided blonde, came out from behind her counter. She had been protected from the machine gun fire by an angle of the wall, but she was as white as a sheet. Police whistles were shrieking outside, and a radio patrol siren sounded as Ed leaped over toward the cashier. "Quick," he shouted. "Those two men standing near me when this began—did you see where they went?"

She nodded, stammered, finally gasped out: "T-they ran out the back way as s-soon as it started."

Ed's eyes were bleak as he turned to confront the two uniformed patrolmen who flung themselves out of a radio car at the curb and rushed into the restaurant. They saw Ed's guns, broke their stride, pawing wildly at their own revolvers. Ed slid his forty-fives back in their holsters, said to the cops: "It's all right. I'm not a bandit. You'll find your men out in that sedan— but I don't think they'll be able to talk much!"

The cops weren't convinced. They had their guns out by this time, and advanced upon Ed grimly. The cashier exclaimed: "No, no. This man is all right. It's he who shot those bandits. If it hadn't been for him, we'd all have been killed!"

Ed flashed her a smile of thanks, motioned to the cops to follow him. They went outside to the sedan just as a police car pulled up. A big, square-jawed man of commanding appearance with a lot of gold braid on his police uniform got out of the squad car; the two cops with Ed saluted him. One of them said: "It looks like a hold-up or something, Captain Lyons. This man here shot it out with the hold-ups."

Captain Lyons glanced searchingly at Ed, said crisply, "Stick close, mister, I'll want to talk to you," and went over to the sedan. Ed followed him, and the two peered into the car. A man lay in the rear, his body twisted on the floor, his head leaning against the edge of the seat. Clutched close to his chest was the machine gun with which he had been shooting. There was a hole in his forehead the size of a quarter. His eyes were open, staring fixed. His face in death was thin, pinched, sharp. In the front seat another man was slumped over the wheel, bloody head on the hands which still clutched its oak rim. Brains and blood were spattered all over. One of Ed's slugs had caught him in the ear. On the far side of the car were a straight line of bullet holes in the frame. Ed's two automatics had cut a line of death across the car, taking both men in its path.

Captain Lyons grunted. "Some shooting—and against a machine gun! Forty-fives, two of them—I count ten holes here, and two shots for these guys." He swung on Ed. "You do it all by yourself?"

Ed nodded. "I carry two of them."

"License?"

Ed nodded again, produced a wallet, opened it, extracted two sheets of paper. One was a license to carry firearms in the state of Pennsylvania, the other was a license to act as a private detective in the same state. Ed had private detective licenses in a dozen states. Long ago, the routine of his acrobatic juggling performances on the stage had begun to become more or less boring to Ed Race's restless temperament. It was at that time that he had begun to seek a side line that would afford him the excitement that his nervous energy craved as an outlet. And he had found it in the avocation of crime detection. His true name, in the past few years, had become as well known and as well hated by underworld crooks as his stage name was known and admired by the theatre-going public.

Captain Lyons saw the name on the licenses and whistled. "I've heard of you, of course...." They moved out of the way for a pair of interns, carrying a stretcher, who had just arrived in an ambulance. "But I didn't think even you were good enough to shoot it out with a machine gun!"

Ed shrugged. "If you had practiced with guns as long as I have, Captain, you'd be just as good. Right now, I'm interested in two men who were trying to take me for a ride before this happened, and in a woman who tried a five-thousand-dollar song-and-dance act on me. I'll give you their descriptions and you send out an alarm."

Swiftly he described the woman and the two men and Lyons dispatched a cop to a telephone. "Have them put it on the seven-state teletype" he ordered. "Those birds will be well on their way by this time, if they're wise! Notify all state police and suburban police departments by radio. Get going. I want those three!"

He turned to Ed. "Any idea what this is all about? Why were they after you?"

Ed was puzzled. "Frankly, I don't understand. I'm to appear at the Partages Theatres starting tomorrow, and I'm also here on a little confidential business for Leon Partages, my boss.

But the business hardly seems to warrant anything like this. Maybe Semple, the theatre manager, can tell us something. He's supposed to meet me at the Carroll town Hotel. Let's call him."

Lyons nodded, and they had started into the restaurant for a 'phone when the captain suddenly halted Ed, murmuring: "Hold it. Here's Bannister."

A limousine was slowing up alongside the gangster's sedan, and a tall man in dinner coat and black felt hat was stepping off the running board, looking with curiosity at the police cars, the ambulance, the crowd that had gathered and which was literally blocking the street.

Ed frowned, asked: "Who's he?"

Lyons laughed. "I forgot you're a stranger. Everybody knows Flint Bannister. He's the political boss of Carrolltown County; owns most of the state politically. He's just had himself appointed Commissioner of Public Works."

Bannister descended from the limousine and headed directly for Lyons. His lively, shrewd eyes flicked over Ed Race for a moment, then rested on the captain. "What's happened here, Lyons? Who's shooting up our city?"

Lyons greeted him respectfully, swiftly told him what had happened, introduced Ed Race. Bannister nodded at Ed. "I've heard of you. The Masked Marksman, eh? Well, you certainly did a good job. It's a good thing you cleaned those gunmen up, or they'd have got away—and the administration would have had a tough time at the coming election. The city owes you a vote of thanks, Race."

"That's fine, Mr. Bannister," Ed said drily. "Now if you'll

excuse us, Captain Lyons and I have a little business to attend to.... We want to see if we can get a line on the other eggs who had a hand in this."

"Other eggs? You mean those two men and the woman that Lyons mentioned? You think they were linked with these gunmen?"

"I sure do. It would be too much of a coincidence to think that this shooting just happened."

"How do you figure to get a line on them?"

"We're going to call up Harry Semple, the manager of the Carrolltown Theatre," Lyons told Bannister, "and see if he knows anything. Race here was supposed to meet him."

"I see," Bannister interrupted. "Well, go ahead. I wish you luck. Too bad about those innocent victims inside. Come and see me tomorrow, Race. I want to do something for you!"

Bannister let them go and returned to his limousine. Ed's eyes followed the political boss thoughtfully until the limousine had turned the corner, then he went inside with Lyons, got the number of the Carrolltown Hotel. "I want to talk to Harry Semple. This is Mr. Race. Semple was to meet me in a room which was reserved in my name."

"Certainly, Mr. Race. Mr. Semple has been expecting you." In a moment Ed was connected with the manager of the Partages Theatre. Semple's voice came to him excitedly: "Mr. Race! Thank God you're here! I was afraid something would happen to you...."

"How come?" Ed asked abruptly. "What were you afraid of?"

"Why—I—er—I don't know." Semple was suddenly cautious

stammering. "I—er—just was worried. Can you come right up here, Mr. Race? I—I'd like to talk to you personally. These telephone wires, you know."

"I'll be right over, Semple," Ed told him crisply. "You stick in that room."

"I will, Mr. Race, I surely will!"

Ed hung up, said to Lyons who was standing at his elbow: "Semple knows something. I'm going up there. Want to come?"

Lyons looked over the scene of wreckage in the restaurant. "I've got to stick here a few minutes until I've gotten this mess kind of cleared up. You go ahead. I'll follow in a few minutes. If you learn anything important from Semple, call me here."

Ed nodded, went out of the restaurant, and crossed the street. The taxicab with his bags was still waiting. The driver grinned at him weakly: "Gee! I thought they got you for a minute, when that Tommy gun opened up. An' I says to myself: 'Mr. Twiggens'—that's my name, Twiggens—I says to myself: 'Mr. Twiggens, here's where you lose ninety cents waiting time!' Then when I seen you come out, I was relieved...."

Ed broke in impatiently: "All right, Twiggens. You take me to the Carrolltown Hotel—quick!"

He got into the cab. Twiggens made a U-turn and headed up Main Street. "Gee," he said over his shoulder, "that was some shooting. It was the best shooting I seen since I rode with Teddy Roosevelt's Rough Riders. Yeah, that was—"

"Listen," Ed interrupted. "You were out there all the time. Did you see that woman come out—the one I went into the restaurant with?"

"Sure I seen her. Say, she has a swell shape, that momma has. An' she knows it, too. I says to myself—"

"Did you see where she went, or what she did when she came out?"

"Sure, I seen where she went. I watched her go down to the corner. A shape like that is worth watching, I'll tell the world. It ain't often—"

Ed gritted his teeth. "Are you going to tell me where she went?"

Twiggens skillfully turned a corner, said: "Sure, sure. She walked kind of fast down to the corner, and a big limousine picked her up and went hell bent for leather down Main Street. You'll laugh when I tell whose limousine it was. You'll never guess—"

"Don't tell me it was Mr. Bannister's limousine!"

"That's what I'm tellin' you, mister. No one else's! An' then you could of knocked me over with a feather when the limousine pulls back here just a couple of minutes ago, an' Bannister himself is inside it—but there ain't no sign of the dame! Boy, he's a lucky stiff with a dame like that. I wish't this was a limousine instead of a hack. Then, maybe, she'd ride with me. I could go for that baby in a big way. I ain't so old, yet, that I couldn't—"

He had swung in to the curb under the canopy of the Carrolltown Hotel. Ed opened the door, leaped out. He handed the driver a five dollar bill. "Here, pop. I don't doubt you could go for her—even if you did ride with Roosevelt. Now listen.... You drive right back to that restaurant and tell Captain Lyons what you just told me. Understand? And then—you hurry here and I'll give you another five-spot. How's that?"

Twiggens pocketed the five dollar bill.

"Sure, mister!… But how about the clock? It says a dollar twenty—"

Ed groaned, pulled out two singles and passed them over. "Now scram!"

Twiggens bobbed his head in delight. "That's fine, mister. That makes the five clear profit. Now I can make the down payment on one of them new auto radios…."

Ed left him in the middle of the sentence, went into the hotel. At the desk he asked: "What room is Mr. Semple in? My name is Race."

The clerk gave him the register to sign, then handed him a key. "Four-nineteen, Mr. Race. Mr. Semple has the other key. You want your bags brought up?"

"Leave them here for the present," Ed told him. "I'm in a hurry."

He crossed to the elevator, went up to the fourth floor. He knocked at 419 but got no answer. Frowning, he inserted the key in the lock, stepped into the room. There was a large double bed in the center, a dresser against the wall, a radio in one corner, and a bathroom door at the far end. On the bed lay a man's hat. Otherwise the room was vacant.

Ed walked around the bed, looked in the closet, found nothing, then went over to the bathroom and pushed the door open. Semple was in the bathroom. He was in the tub, and his feet were sticking up over the side at a grotesque angle. His head was down in the tub, and blood had discolored the white porcelain. Semple was dead. His head had been bashed in. There was no weapon in sight.

Ed made sure the theatre manager was dead. He had met Semple once before, when the man had been manager of a theatre in another town; knew that Semple was married, had two children. His lips were a tight line as he went out of the bathroom, picked up the hat on the bed and saw that the initials on the brim were "H. S."

The telephone rang. Ed picked it up mechanically, said: "Yes?"

An excited voice said: "Hey, mister! This is Twiggens!"

Ed said tonelessly: "Well?"

"Say, mister, I'm phoning from a drug store at Portland and Fifth Streets. Just as you went in the hotel, I drove off, and who do you think I seen come out of the side entrance of the hotel?"

"Never mind the guessing games!" Ed snapped.

"All right, mister, you don't have to get sore. I seen that dame you was asking me about—you know, the one with the shape—"

"Yes," Ed rapped. He clutched the receiver hard.

"She was coming out wit' two other men, an' one of them limped. They flagged me, and I acted dumb, picked them up. They got off at the corner of Portland and Fifth, and started to walk. They walked two blocks, and went in the back way of a big house. Guess whose house...."

Ed was almost weeping. "Damn it, quit those guessing games. Snap it up!"

"All right, all right. I was just trying to tell you. It's the house of—say, how much will it be worth to you to know?"

Ed groaned. "Ten dollars. And when I see you I'm going to take a sock out of you."

"Then I ain't agoin' to tell you. I don't like being socked...."

"All right, I give up. Ten dollars, and no socks. Whose house?"

"Mr. Flint Bannister's!" Twiggens chuckled. "When do I get the ten?"

"Right now! You wait right where you are. I'll be there before you can leave the booth!"

"Okay, and don't forget, no socks—"

Ed hung up, raced out of the room. He punched the button till the elevator came up. Down at the desk he asked the clerk: "Did anyone go up to see Mr. Semple before I came?"

"No sir."

"Did anybody go up to the fourth floor?"

"Why, yes.... A lady and two men."

"Okay. You call this number—" he gave the clerk the number of the restaurant, which he had jotted down, "and ask for Captain Lyons. Tell him to meet me at Flint Bannister's house at once. Understand? I've no time to 'phone him myself. And then you call headquarters and have them send a couple of men over. Mr. Semple has been murdered in four-nine-teen!"

The clerk gasped, grew pale. But Ed wasn't there to see him. He was already out the door, hailing a cab. "Fifth and Portland!" he snapped. "And don't spare the gas!"

Portland and Fifth was about a mile and a half from the center of town, in the more expensive residential section. Twiggens was waiting as he had promised. Ed paid off his own driver, gripped Twiggens by the sleeve. "All right, take me to that house!"

Twiggens held back. "Ten bucks, you said."

Impatiently, Ed peeled off a ten dollar bill, handed it over. He got into the cab, while Twiggens got behind the wheel and pulled away from the curb. "You know, mister, it looked funny, the way that dame came out with those guys. She was in the middle, sort of pulling back and crying…. One of the guys tells her to shut up, or he'd smack her. Then she shut up."

"I see," Ed said thoughtfully. "Listen, Wiggins—"

"It ain't Wiggins, mister—it's Twiggens—T-w-i—"

"Okay, Twiggens. My apologies. You take me to the back entrance where they went in, and then you go around the front and wait for Captain Lyons. When he comes, you tell him everything you told me."

The rear entrance of Bannister's house was on Fairmount Street. It was a large place, and there was a driveway that ran from the front through to the rear of the lot, with a *porte-cochère* at the side of the house. Ed left the cab and walked up the driveway. It was dark here, but lights from several windows in the house glowed dimly through drawn shades.

Ed stopped close to the rear door, listened for movement within, shrugged, and took out a bunch of passkeys. The second try clicked the lock…. He stepped into a pantry just behind the kitchen. There was no one in the kitchen, though it was brightly lit. He passed through into a hall, heard voices upstairs. He moved down along the hall, silently, looked into two empty rooms, the doors of which were wide open. The voices were still coming from upstairs, and Ed, though he couldn't catch words, recognized a feminine voice—that of Elsie Robinson!

He went up the stairs cautiously, reached the upper landing, and stopped, staring through the open door into a bedroom. Elsie Robinson stood in the room, with her back to the wall, one hand at her throat, the other at her breast. Facing her, with his left side to the door through which Ed looked, was the tall, poised figure of Flint Bannister. He was still wearing his distinguished-looking evening clothes. In his right hand was a small nickel-plated revolver, to the muzzle of which was attached a silencer. At the right of the woman stood the second of the two men who had tried to hold Ed up in the restaurant; he, too, had a gun.

Bannister was saying in a cool, composed voice: "It's too bad, Elsie, but I can't give up a million and a half dollars just because you suddenly become squeamish!"

Elsie Robinson was no longer the hard, self-assured woman that she had been in the restaurant. Her eyes were wide with fear, and her lips were trembling. Ed, from the hallway, could see the pallor of her cheeks through the rouge.

She said tremblingly: "B-but you didn't tell me there was going to be murder. Y-you just hired me to stop Ed Race at the station, and buy him off. I—I thought that Croner here, and Smiley, were just going to take him away and make him report 'okay' to Partages—so he'd sell the theatre…. B-but instead of that, you had those men in the car, with the machine gun—"

Croner snarled: "Sure! You didn't think a guy like Race could be handled like any ordinary egg? When he refused to take that dough you offered him, there was only one thing to do—bop him! We had the two boys with the chopper along for insurance, on account of how Race is supposed to be pretty good with a gun—and it was damn lucky they were along, or we'd be in the can by now."

Bannister smiled thinly. "You see, Elsie, there's no use getting an attack of conscience at this late date. We've got to go through with it. The only chance of our putting the deal through is to get this man Race on the spot. He's got to be put out of the way before tomorrow morning, because, by then, he'll learn that the city council has condemned the Partages Theatre property for a million and a half, and he'll wire Partages not to sell. Semple is out of the way—Race is our only danger. Now I want you to 'phone him, tell him that you can give him the low-down if he'll come to meet you alone. From what I've heard of him, he'll rise to the bait. And Croner and Smiley will be there to take care of him—only this time, they'll be sure to shoot before he sees them!"

Elsie Robinson shrank back against the wall. "I won't do it!" she exclaimed. "I won't. If I'd known you were a bunch of murderers I would never have taken the job. I thought you were just putting over a clever deal—having the property condemned by the city for a million and a half, and buying it up from Partages for two hundred and fifty thousand, but—"

Bannister took a short step forward. "You mean that, Elsie? You won't go through with it?"

"I won't! I won't have anything to do with m-murder!"

Bannister said to Croner: "Well, I guess that's that. Take her away, Croner. You know what to do with her."

Croner grinned nastily. "And how! Come on, girlie—one last ride!"

She opened her mouth to scream, and Croner hit her. The blow sent her head back against the wall, she reeled, almost stumbled. Croner caught her by the arm, half carried her toward the door. At that moment Ed stepped forward, his hands going to his two shoulder holsters.

But before he could move a gun barrel jammed into his back. He stiffened, half turned, saw the game-legged man, Smiley.

Smiley had come out of an open door on the other side of the hall behind Ed. The limping man's teeth showed in a vicious smile. "Wise guy, huh! Take it easy, bo, and walk inside. Don't make no funny moves!"

Bannister and Croner stared, gaping at Ed as he stepped into the room under the muzzle of Smiley's gun. Bannister exclaimed: "Good man, Smiley!"

Smiley grinned. "I was in the bathroom, and I come out an' seen this mugg in the hall. So I steps up in back of him, an' here he is!"

Bannister faced Ed Race, said softly: "You've been an awful nuisance, Race. It'll be a pleasure to lose you!"

Elsie Robinson was leaning against the wall where Croner had let her go. She cried: "They'll kill us both, Mr. Race! God, they'll kill us—"

Croner gave her a vicious backhanded slap that sent her staggering, and Smiley, behind Ed, chuckled. Ed felt the muzzle of the gun in his back wobble a little as Smiley laughed, and—he swung into action. His right foot kicked back hard, caught

Smiley in the shin. It was Smiley's good leg, and the gunman yelped, bent over. Ed whirled, his left fist crashed against Smiley's jaw with shattering impact, sending him backward in a heap up against Bannister.

And with a continuous motion, Ed dived into a forward somersault that carried him half way across the room, out of line of the slugs that ripped from Croner's gun. Croner was snarling, firing from the hip, but his target was moving in a whirling somersault of arms and legs. People in vaudeville theatres all over the country had often seen the Masked Marksman do that trick somersault, come out of it, catch the guns he had been juggling, and shoot out the flames of a row of candles, almost before they knew what was happening. Just so did Ed Race now come out of his somersault, with his two forty-fives in his hands, bucking, roaring, as slugs thundered from their muzzles into the body of Croner. Croner was hurled back into the wall as if a hurricane had caught him. His chest seemed to cave in into a bloody ruin as the slugs pounded into him. His mouth fell open, his body slid down the wall to the floor at the feet of Elsie Robinson who stared at the gruesome sight, horribly fascinated.

Almost before he had ceased firing at Croner, Ed swung the gun in his right hand lithely, fired once at Bannister, who had recovered his balance and was pointing the silenced revolver at him. Ed's slug caught Bannister in the mouth, and the politician's face seemed suddenly to dissolve.

Ed stopped shooting, looked around the room bitterly. The only one of the three who was not dead was Smiley, and he was lying on the floor with a broken jaw.

Someone was pounding at the front door, and police whistles were sounding outside. Ed looked across at Elsie Robinson. She was pressing both white-knuckled fists against her breasts, and looking piteously at him.

There was a crash downstairs, and the sound of running feet. Uniformed figures appeared in the room. Captain Lyons stared for a moment, then exclaimed: "Holy Mackerel! Bannister! Was he in this?"

Ed grunted. "It was his plan. Am I right, Elsie?"

She nodded. "Bannister had the City Council condemn the block of buildings where the Partages Theatre is located for a public park. The news of the condemnation was to have been announced tomorrow. The Partages Theatre was valued at a million and a half by the Council, and Bannister wanted to buy it up for two hundred and fifty thousand. He'd have made the difference. He had bribed Semple to advise Partages to sell, but when Semple's conscience began to bother him, Bannister got some of the boys in to threaten him. Then when we learned from Semple that Ed Race was coming—Bannister told me to try to bribe him, too. Semple was going to tell the whole story to Mr. Race, so Croner and Smiley shot him. I was with them—I wanted to quit, but they dragged me over here."

Lyons looked from the moaning form of Smiley on the floor, up to Ed Race. "Well, I'll be damned!" he said.

Elsie Robinson took a timid step forward. "W-what's going to be done t-to me?"

"I think," Ed said, "that you will get off pretty light by turning state's evidence. There's still Smiley to prosecute. What do you say, Lyons?"

The captain nodded, started to speak—he was interrupted by a voice from the doorway. "Well, gosh all! I ain't never seen so much blood since I rode with Teddy Roosevelt!"

Ed frowned, demanded: "What the hell do you want now, Twiggens?"

The taxi driver shuffled his feet. "Well you see, I was kind of worried about my waitin' time when I heard the shooting…. There's seventy cents on the clock!"

DEATH AT THE MATINEE

TO ED RACE, the proceedings were eminently disgusting. The big man with the pale-green necktie had no business punching the little man in the face that way; and when he tweaked his nose, it wasn't funny at all.

However, the dozen or so people who sat in the otherwise empty orchestra of the Clyde Theatre were laughing their sides off, so Ed thought that maybe it was his own sense of humor that was going stale. Those dozen men were the typical Broadway about-towners who invariably showed up at Monday morning rehearsals, and they ought to know what was good in vaudeville and what wasn't.

Ed shrugged and slouched glumly in his first-row seat between Leon Partages and Jimmy Oglethorpe. Partages, the owner of the Clyde, Ed's boss, and the boss of the whole countrywide Partages Circuit, seemed to think that it was funny as the dickens for Frankie Brown to be smacking Harry Brown every time Harry made a wisecrack. So did Jimmy Oglethorpe, Ed's young friend from Washington. Jimmy was one of Mr. Hoover's Special Agents. He had just come in to New York on government business, and Ed Race had been showing him around in his spare time.

Ed's gun-juggling and acrobatic act was the headliner at

the Clyde, and Ed had just finished rehearsing, so he was now watching the other members.

Harry and Frankie Brown, billed as the Two Brownies, finished their routine with a slam-bang, and bowed themselves off the stage.

Partages was laughing deep in his fat belly, and he turned to Ed, said between gulps of laughter: "What do you think of it, Eddie? Harry was okay as a comic by himself, but taking his brother into the act was a stroke of genius. Now he gets off all his gags with an extra kick."

Ed made a sour face. "Sorry, Mr. Partages, but I can't see the fun of it. Slapstick comedy never appealed to me." He turned to Jimmy Oglethorpe, on his right. "What do you think, Jimmy-the-G-Man? Was that act funny?"

Jimmy Oglethorpe was a young, clear-eyed, healthy-cheeked husky. He had been an all-around athlete at Leland University, then had studied law and made the Federal Bureau of Investigation. He was laughing heartily, and applauding. He looked at Ed Race, grinned and said: "Go on, you old clam, why don't you open up and give the boys a hand. I think they're good!"

Ed threw up his hands in despair. "Everybody to his taste," he said. "Some people even like tripe!"

Jimmy Oglethorpe looked at his watch, exclaimed: "Wow! Eleven forty-five, and I've got to meet my regional chief at noon. I got to go, Ed!"

Partages waved to them. "Run along, boys. See you for the afternoon show, Eddie. Remember—your curtain call's at four-fifteen sharp! And I still think the Two Brownies are good."

Ed made a face, pushed Jimmy Oglethorpe up the aisle. In the lobby, a little old lady in a black bonnet was buying two tickets at the Advance Sale window. She had a copy of *Variety* under one arm, and she was holding the two tickets in her left hand, her big black handbag in her right, and at the same time trying to manage the change of twenty dollars which the cashier was handing her.

Jimmy Oglethorpe gripped Ed Race's arm in sudden excitement, exclaimed under his breath: "Wow!"

Ed gave him a queer look. "Whatsamatter, Jimmy? Your long-lost mother?"

The young F.B.I. man hastily drew Ed Race into a far corner of the lobby. "Listen, Ed," he whispered, "that's a dame that F.B.I. has been looking for all over the country. What a break for me! Look, Ed, I've got to trail her. But I also have to meet my regional chief, Sam Kerwin, in Pennsylvania Station. He's coming in from Washington at twelve o'clock. Be a good guy, Ed, and go down to meet him. Will you?"

Ed nodded. "All right, Sherlock. As long as it's in the nation's service. I've met Kerwin. What'll I tell him—that you're off after a dame?"

"You tell him that I'm on the trail of Mrs. Porter. He'll know what that means. Take him to your hotel, and tell him to wait there for my call. I'll 'phone in the first chance I get."

Ed caught the edge of Oglethorpe's excitement, and nodded quickly. "Okay, Jimmy. Better get going—she's on her way out."
JIMMY LEFT him following after the old lady. Ed watched them for a moment, saw how skillfully Jimmy Oglethorpe faded

into the Broadway crowd behind his quarry. She was moving south on Broadway, and Ed had to go south, too, so he trailed along down to the corner. The old lady stopped for a moment, buffered by the crowd, opened her copy of *Variety* to an inside page, tore out an item from an end column, and threw the rest of the paper in the big waste-paper receptacle alongside the lamp post. Then she flagged a cab, and Jimmy Oglethorpe got into another, following her.

Ed Race turned away, walked down another block and entered the subway. At Pennsylvania Station he was just in time to catch the crowd disembarking from the twelve o'clock train.

Sam Kerwin was much older than Jimmy Oglethorpe, with the poise which years of experience bring to the trained manhunter. On the way up to Ed's hotel, they exchanged reminiscences. Kerwin had once been a first-grade detective on the New York Police Force, and had occasion to know Ed Race's peculiar abilities. To the theatre-going public, Ed was known as "The Masked Marksman—The Man Who Can Make Guns Talk." On the stage he performed feats of acrobatics and marksmanship that left the audience breathless at his sheer skill. He juggled with six heavy forty-five calibre, hair-trigger revolvers instead of with Indian clubs, and he could catch those revolvers in midair, fire them at the flames of a row of candles thirty feet across the stage—and put out the flames.

But it was off stage that Kerwin had come to know Ed Race. For Ed's overflowing nervous energy had caused him to seek an avocation that would furnish more excitement than he found in the theatre. That avocation was the detection of crime. He had licenses in a dozen states as a private detective, and his bewildering skill with the two forty-fives that he always carried in his twin shoulder holsters had made his name well-known—and favorably—to the police of dozens of cities; and well-hated by a good slice of the underworld.

So he and Kerwin had much to talk about, and they did their talking over a series of old-fashioneds in the bar of the Longmont Hotel. That is, Ed had the old-fashioneds, while Kerwin drank coffee. It was almost two hours later when Kerwin looked at the time worriedly. "Look here, Ed," he said, "there's something queer about this. Oglethorpe should have called in by this time. That old lady can't be traveling around in taxicabs for two hours; and if she stopped anywhere, Jimmy should have been able to get in a call. I'm worried."

Ed sipped his old-fashioned. "Don't tell me, if it's impertinent, Kerwy, but who is that old lady, anyway?"

Kerwin frowned. "I could get canned for telling you, but what the hell. Mrs. Porter is the mother of a certain bird that's wanted for mail robbery and murder in the Middle West. They call him Teddy 'Slicer.' Heard the name?"

Ed nodded. "Read about it in the papers, that's all. They say he got the name because he slices them in half with a tommy gun."

"That's the one!" Kerwin said grimly. "He isn't satisfied with just killing them; he sprays that typewriter so that his victims are literally cut in half. I've seen the bodies."

"Nice man," Ed commented. "How could he have a mother?"

"He has. We found who she was, but we don't think Teddy Slicer knows that we know. We put a tail on her, hoping that at some time or other her loving son would communicate with her. We drew a blank for ten days, and then suddenly she disappeared. Our man out there got careless, and she slipped right out of sight. That's what I was coming to New York to meet Jimmy for. The country is being combed for her. We figure that where she is, her son will be. I was coming here to work the New York sector. And what happens when I arrive, but you tell me that Jimmy has her spotted already!"

Ed was thoughtful. "You think she came here to join her son?"

"We don't know what to think. She's such a quiet, mouse-like old lady that we don't even think she knows what her son is doing. But then, again, we may be all wrong."

Ed finished his old-fashioned. "Look here, Kerwy," he said suddenly, "Jimmy may have walked into something hot. You can't leave this place, because he may call in any minute. All right, you stay here and keep working on your coffee, while I go out and see if I can pick up the trail of the two of them."

Kerwin nodded. "I've got to wait, anyway, because I've 'phoned for some more agents to meet me here. They'll be arriving in a little while. You call me here in half an hour, whether you have any success or not."

ED LEFT him and took a cab back to the Clyde. His first stop was at the trash receptacle at the corner, where Mrs. Porter had thrown her copy of *Variety*. Surprisingly, it was empty.

He went into the corner cigar store and entered a 'phone booth. He had Kerwin paged in the Longmont bar.

"Any word from Jimmy Oglethorpe yet?" he asked.

"Not a thing, Ed. What have you got?"

"That old lady," Ed told him, "dropped a copy of *Variety* into the trash can on the corner of Broadway and Forty-sixth. She cut something out of it before she threw it in. The stuff was picked up in a truck before I got here. Can you trace that truck, and have it fished through for the paper? If we can find which clipping she tore out, it may be a lead."

"I'll get right to it," Kerwin told him. "That's an easy one. Call me back after a while."

ED HUNG up, went up the street to the Clyde. In the lobby he went over to the Advance Sale window.

"Howya, Mr. Race?" greeted Mabel, the cashier. "Wanna buy a ticket to your own show?"

"Listen, Mabel," Ed said glumly, "about a quarter to twelve, an old lady bought two tickets, and you gave her change of twenty. Remember?"

"Uh-huh. She wore a funny bonnet. Whatsamatter—you think the twenty was phony? It looked good to me. She bought two tickets in the first row balcony for tonight's show."

"Have you got the twenty?"

Mabel fingered through the bills in the drawer, pulled one out. "Here it is—AA1 and AA3. I always mark the seat numbers in pencil on large bills—just in case of a phony."

Ed took the bill, gave her another twenty for it.

The bill was a Federal Reserve Bank note, issued by the Howard National Bank of New York. Ed sighed with relief as he crinkled it, noted that it was brand new. He strode away from the window, leaving Mabel staring after him in perplexity, and went outside, walked two blocks south and a block east, entered the marble precincts of the Howard National Bank.

A man seated at a desk behind the front railing raised a hand in greeting, and Ed went in, plumped down in a chair. "Hello, Mr. Simonson."

"How are you, Race? I meant to talk to you about your account—"

"Not now, Simonson. I'm in a hurry—a hell of a hurry. Will you do me a favor?"

"Of course—but the limit is ten thousand." Simonson chuckled.

Ed put the twenty-dollar bill on the desk. "I'd like to find out to whom this bill was issued. It's damned important."

Simonson said: "Sit here a minute, huh?"

He took the bill, went in back. In a couple of minutes he returned. "This was one of a bundle of twenties issued to one of our depositors, late yesterday."

Ed leaned forward eagerly. "What's the depositor's name?"

Simonson chuckled again. "You can go right back to where you started this morning, Race. It was issued to the Longmont Hotel—where you stay!"

"Hell!" Ed exclaimed. "I was there less than an hour ago!"

The bank official gave him a queer look. "Is this a runaround or something you're giving me, Race? Did you by any chance get that bill at the Longmont yourself, and bring it in to try me out, by any chance?"

"By any chance," Ed told him primly, "I did not. I'll be seeing you, Simonson—and thanks."

He went out wearily, and got in a cab headed for the Longmont on Forty-eighth. He wondered if he was going through a lot of stewing for nothing. Oglethorpe might be quite safe, still tailing the old lady. But if that were so, the origin of the twenty-dollar bill indicated that the old lady must be staying at the Longmont. In which event, Oglethorpe would have tailed her there, and he would surely have been able to contact Ed and Kerwin in the bar. Something must have happened. Either Oglethorpe had lost the old lady, or else—

At the Longmont Ed paid off the driver and went in through the bar. Kerwin wasn't there.

Ed went up to the desk, and the clerk said: "Message for you, Mr. Race. Mr. Kerwin went down to the city incinerator plant. He says you're to wait for a call from him."

"Okay," Ed said. "Now tell me—have you got anybody registered here by the name of Porter—a little old lady in a funny bonnet—"

"Sure. Room 509, right above your room. It's a double, in the name of Mrs. Porter and Miss Brown."

"Five-O-nine, eh? Okay. If Mr. Kerwin calls, connect me with him up there. Give me the key to that room."

"The key? But, say—"

"Lay off the argument!" Ed snapped. "This is a matter of life and death. I've been here long enough for you to know I'm all right. Hand it over, quick!"

The clerk shrugged. "It's all right with me, Mr. Race. I know you're a private dick. Here's the key. Mrs. Porter is out."

"Did anybody call to see her in the last couple of hours?"

"Why, not that I know of. A lot of people just go up without asking at the desk. She came in a while ago, and, come to think of it, she went out only about a half-hour back, with a man."

"Was he a young fellow, athletic?"

"No. He was a pretty stocky chap, heavy built. I just got a quick look. You know I pay little attention—"

"Too little!" Ed murmured.

"Say!" the clerk exclaimed. "Come to think of it, a young fellow like you describe came in right after Mrs. Porter and asked what room she was in. He showed me a badge. I gave him the number, but I don't know if he went up."

"That's enough, Oscar," Ed said hurriedly. He left the clerk, took the elevator up to five-o-nine.

THERE WAS a "Do Not Disturb" sign on the door, and Ed was careful not to disturb. He inserted the key very quietly, and pushed noiselessly into the room. It was the usual double-room-and-bath of the Longmont, with the layout exactly the same as Ed's room on the floor below—the bed in the center of the room, the bathroom opening off the small foyer.

Ed pushed past the bathroom door, went into the room itself. The shades were all down, and the place was gloomy, but there was enough light to discern what was lying on the bed.

Ed's lips twisted in a grimace of pain, and his eyes assumed a bleak, hard glint. He stepped closer, put out a hand and touched Jimmy Oglethorpe's face. It was still warm, but the feel of death was there. That gesture of Ed's was really not necessary, for it could be seen at a glance that Oglethorpe was dead. He was lying on his back. His coat was wide open, and his natty blue shirt was stained a deep red around the heart. Blood had seeped down from the wound onto the inside of his coat, and through the coat onto the bed.

Ed bent closer, inspected the wound. There were powder burns around it on the shirt. Oglethorpe had been shot at close range. His face was composed, as if he had not expected or anticipated the shot which ended his life.

Ed Race's eyes clouded. He felt a lump in his throat, and

he gulped. "God, Jimmy," he murmured, looking down at the youthful face, "you had plenty of life in you yet!"

Abruptly he turned away from the bed, let his eyes wander over the room. The clothes closet was open, showing coats and dresses hung in orderly rows. On a chair near the window were a brassiere, a pair of step-ins, and a pair of stockings. On the floor at the foot of the chair was a pair of high-heeled pumps.

Ed noticed two traveling bags, which had evidently been delivered to the Longmont from the railroad station by the Transfer Company. They bore tags reading: "Mrs. Arabella Porter, River City, Wisconsin, to Longmont Hotel, New York." And the other: "Miss Sylvia Brown, River City, Wisconsin, to Longmont Hotel, New York."

Ed didn't touch the bags. He moved through the room, went into the foyer, and opened the bathroom door. A light summer bathrobe was hanging on the hook in the door. A tube of cold cream, with cap off, lay on the washbasin. The bathtub was empty. The shower sheet, however, was drawn across the stand-up shower, built into the wall alongside the tub.

Ed reached over, pulled the shower sheet away, and uttered a gasp of surprise.

A girl was huddled on the floor of the shower. Her skin gleamed white and soft, and she did not stir. She had no clothes at all, and her body was so still that at first Ed though she was dead. He bent closer, heard her steady breathing. Gently he lifted her out. She was not wounded, had just fainted, apparently. Ed put her feet on the cold tile floor, and she suddenly opened her eyes, shrank from him with sudden, instinctive fear.

Ed took down the bathrobe, put it around her, and said: "It's all right, Miss Brown. I won't hurt you."

She snuggled into the bathrobe, stood there small and fragile, the fear slowly fading from her face as she read the kindliness in his eyes.

"Who—who are you?" she asked.

"The name is Race," Ed told her. "I'm a kind of detective."

Suddenly, blind horror took possession of the girl's sensitive face. Her eyes filled with recollection and dread. She moaned: "The dead man! He shot him!" She swayed, and Ed put out a quick hand to steady her. She slumped in his arms.

Ed said crisply: "Come now, Miss Brown, this is no time to faint. You know a man's been killed. Who killed him?"

He felt her slim body quivering in his arms. "Oh God, it—it was terrible. Mrs. Porter's son killed him. He shot him. I—I was in the shower when Mrs. Porter came home, and a few minutes later someone knocked at the door. She opened it, and two men came in. I—I didn't come out, but you can hear everything that's said inside, through the ventilator shaft. One man with a beery voice was saying: 'Keep your mitts in the air, punk!' And then Mrs. Porter cried out: 'My son! What has happened? What are you going to do to this young man?'"

THE GIRL was still trembling, and Ed patted her on the shoulder. "Go on, Miss Brown. You're doing all right. Get it over with quick."

"I—I remember every word they said. The man with the beery voice was snarling. He said: 'Mom, what was the idea of coming to New York? Now you got this punk of a G-Man on my trail!'

And Mrs. Porter was crying. She said: 'I saw your picture, son, and wanted to see how you were doing.' Then she asked: 'Why should he be on your trail, son? Have you done wrong?' And the man said brutally: 'Well, you got to know it sometime. I'm wanted for murder. They call me Teddy Slicer. How do you like that, Mom?' Then they talked for a couple of minutes, and I heard the young man arguing with him, and suddenly there was the sound of the shot, and Mrs. Porter screamed: 'You've killed him!' The man with the beery voice laughed, and said: 'Come on, Mom, we got to get out of this. You wouldn't turn your own son in for a murderer—or would you, maybe?'

"After that they were silent for a while, and then I heard them both go out. And then—I must have fainted!"

Ed asked bitterly: "You didn't get a look at this man with the beery voice?"

She shook her head.

"Do you know who he is?"

She hesitated, then said slowly: "God help me, I think I do!"

Ed shook her. "Who?"

But there was no response. She had fainted again. Ed cursed grimly. He lifted her in his arms, started to carry her into the bedroom, then remembered what lay on the bed, and stood in indecision a moment. The telephone inside rang—Ed had to do something with her, so he put her on the floor and placed the bath mat under her head. He went in past the body of Oglethorpe on the bed, and answered the 'phone. It was Kerwin.

"That you, Race?" said the G-Man. "Say, we found that copy of *Variety*. How are you doing?"

"Not so well," Ed said quietly. "Can you take it, Kerwin?"

There was a slight pause. "You mean—Jimmy Oglethorpe?"

"Yes, Kerwin."

"Dead?"

"Yes."

There was a long silence. Then from the other end a muted whisper: "God! The poor kid!"

Ed said in a flat voice: "I know how you feel, Kerwin. I feel the same. The kid was a good friend."

"How did he get it, Race?"

"He was shot right here in room 509 of the Longmont. He traced Mrs. Porter here, and her son must have spotted him, and got the drop on him. He brought him in here and killed him. There's a girl here, who heard everything from the bathroom. But she's fainted, and I can't get anything more from her. Porter took his mother out of here."

"You have no idea who or where he is?"

"I have a damn good idea, Kerwin, but I've got to check it first; got to be damned sure. What about that clipping from *Variety?*"

"There's about three inches torn from the last two columns of page five. I can't get a copy of the paper to see what the item is. We're way out here at the wrong end of Brooklyn. But you buy one and take a look. I'll come right in to the Longmont."

"Make it the Clyde Theatre, Kerwin. I have to go on at four-fifteen. And I'll want you there, if I'm not mistaken."

He waited till Kerwin had hung up, then signaled the operator and said: "Send up Halloran, the house dick."

He went back in the bathroom, tried to revive the girl with water, but failed. She was evidently suffering from severe mental shock.

Halloran came in while he was working over her, and Ed explained the situation to him as briefly as possible.

The redheaded house detective of the Longmont threw up his hands. "Ye gods and little fishes, Race! This is the ninth homicide that's taken place in the hotel since you came to live in it!"

"Lay off," Ed said curtly. "That poor kid was a good friend!"

"Geez, I'm sorry, Race," Halloran said contritely. "I didn't know."

"All right, Halloran. I'm going now. If the girl comes to, try to get her to talk, and 'phone me at the Clyde. When the homicide men get here, tell them this is an F.B.I. case, and to wait for Kerwin."

DOWN IN the lobby, Ed bought a copy of *Variety*, turned to page five. The item in the upper corner contained two pictures, and an announcement that Harry Brown had teamed up with a partner, to be known as Frankie Brown, and that the two would appear on the Partages Circuit as the Two Brownies. The pictures were likenesses of the Two Brownies.

Ed strode out of the hotel, didn't bother with a cab, but walked the short distance to the Clyde. It was without doubt that clipping which had brought Mrs. Porter to New York. According to the girl, Mrs. Porter had said that she had seen her son's picture in the paper. She had bought two tickets to the evening performance. It added up. One of the Browns must be

Teddy Slicer. It couldn't be Harry, because his actions for the past ten years were all accounted for.

Ed turned in to the stage entrance of the Clyde, headed back toward the dressing rooms, disregarding the various greetings that were thrown his way. Norma Maitland had the stage, and the audience was giving her a good hand on her first number. Ed looked around but did not see either of the Brownies. He stopped before their dressing room, nudged his shoulder holsters just a bit farther forward, and knocked at the door. There was no answer. He knocked again, harder. A voice growled: "It ain't our cue. What the hell do you want?"

"Can I come in?"

"No!" The voice went on, snapping at someone else in the room: "Lock that door. We don't want no visitors!"

Ed heard a step approaching the door, put a hand to the knob and pushed the door open quickly. He was in the room and had the door shut in a trice, and stood with his back to it facing the tense tableau there. Harry Brown was on his way toward the door to lock it, and stood poised on one foot, stopped in mid-stride.

In the center of the small room stood the little old lady in the black bonnet. Her face was streaked with the marks of tears, and her narrow shoulders were shrunken so that she seemed to cower. In the corner, seated facing them on the dressing table bench, was Frankie Brown. His thickly jowled face was twisted into an unnatural smile, and his small eyes were fixed on Ed. But Ed was looking at the thing he held in his lap. It was a

Thompson submachine gun, and Frankie Brown held it so that it covered the room.

Ed said to him flatly: "You're Teddy Slicer!"

Brown nodded, still smiling twistedly. "That's me, pal. And what might your name be? I always like the names of the guys I'm gonna slice in two."

"The name is Race," Ed told him. "You were certainly a sap to let your picture be taken and printed in *Variety*." Ed turned to the old lady. "You recognized his picture, didn't you?"

She nodded, her eyes welling once more with tears. "He'd had his face changed, and that was why he wasn't afraid to have his picture printed. But I recognized his eyes—the same eyes his father had. I had to come to New York to see how he was doing in vaudeville. I—I didn't know the Federal men were following me."

Teddy Slicer sneered, shifted a little on the bench so that the muzzle of the Thompson was pointing squarely at Ed's stomach. "I got to go now," he said. "Things is getting too hot around here. The boys are right on my tail. Mom, you go on out."

Mrs. Porter twisted her thin hands. "No, no! Stop these killings. You—"

She stopped, as Teddy Slicer half rose from the bench, snarling. "I said get out! Or do you want to see them get it?"

ED INTERRUPTED mildly: "Excuse me for asking, but how do you figure to get away with a shooting right in the heart of New York?"

The Slicer was leering at him. "I got it all figured out, wise guy. It's so smart, I got to tell somebody, and there's damn few I can talk to nowadays. See, after I slice you birds in two, I'll run outta here and yell: 'Help! They're murderin' my brother!' He ain't my brother, see, but they think he is. Then while everything is upset, I hop a cab to the ferry across Forty-second."

He was beaming at his own cleverness.

Ed beamed back at him. "That's damned clever, Mister Slicer. But pardon me if I ask another question. Do you mind?"

"Go ahead. I like to talk to an intelligent guy like you."

"I just wanted to know why you insist on killing Harry Brown here. He gave you an alibi, took you into the show, made you his partner. You might have been set here, safe from detection, if there hadn't been a fluke. Why do you have to kill him?"

Harry Brown was standing tensely near the door, looking from the Slicer to Ed Race. The Slicer growled: "Sure, he done all that. But he didn't do it because he liked it. He did it because he was afraid for his kid sister. I told him he better fix me up, or I'd slit his kid sister's throat. I made him give out the announcement that he was taking me in as partner, an' then when we started to rehearse for the act it was too late for him to sell me out—he'd have been an accessory. See?"

Ed looked almost unbelievingly at Harry Brown. "You let him bulldoze you like that?"

Harry Brown hung his head. "You see, Ed, he's—legally married to Sylvia. She never took his name. The day after she married him we found out what he really was."

Ed said slowly: "I see."

The Slicer got up from his seat. "All right, Mom, I changed

my mind. You get over in that closet. I'll have to lock you in so you can't be tempted to give me away when I run out—"

The old lady drew herself up, wiped the tears from her eyes, and faced the Slicer. "No! You'll have to kill me, too! I—don't—want—to live anymore!" Deliberately, slowly, she started to walk toward him.

The Slicer snarled at her. "Get back! You want me to give it to you, too? Get back, I tell you!" He swung the muzzle of the tommy toward her. And in the split second that the muzzle was moved, while the Slicer's eyes were off him, Ed Race's two hands crossed over his chest with the unbelievable speed of light.

The Slicer's hand was already tautening on the trip of the tommy, pointed at his own mother, when Ed's two guns roared in thunderous rhythm, deafening everybody in the small room, reverberating through the thin partitions out into the backstage section of the theatre.

The Slicer's body was hurled around as if by a cyclone. Great gouts of blood appeared on his chest. Ed's slugs thrust him against the wall, dead before he hit it.

Mrs. Porter was standing, white-faced, with her back to the wall. Harry Brown had stood transfixed, through all the fusillade, right where he had been at the start. Now, as the thunderous echoes of the detonations of the heavy forty-fives died away, Ed said in a tight voice: "I think it's better for your sister to be a widow."

Then he looked at the little old lady. "I'm sorry, Mrs. Porter, that it had to be in your presence—"

She closed her eyes, shook her head slightly. "I had rather it happened this way. It is dreadful for a mother to see her own son shot to death, but I bear you no hate. Indeed, I thank you. Now I can be assured that my flesh and blood shall not be the cause of other deaths!"

There was a loud shouting and hubbub outside the door. Ed flung it open. The crowd gaped into the room, but Ed shooed them away. From the direction of the stage entrance he saw Kerwin and two of his men running toward them.

"All over?" Kerwin said.

Ed nodded silently. For a moment the two men looked into each other's eyes. Kerwin's eyes clouded. Slowly he took off his hat. Ed did likewise. "In respect to a brave man—Jimmy Oglethorpe!" Kerwin murmured.

"And," Ed Race added, turning to gaze into the smoke-filled dressing room at the straight, frail form of Mrs. Porter, "in respect to a very brave lady." He spoke the last words very softly, so that only Kerwin heard him.